The
Celestial
Connection

The Celestial Connection

by

ROMAN FRANCE

Tale Spin Press
East Coast Division
Maryland

Tale Spin Press
East Coast Division
P.O. Box 2674
Ellicott City, MD 21041-2674

The three principal characters, Bob, Tom, and Clair are pseudonyms, and the names of certain places have been changed; otherwise their accounts are true. Other characters, incidents, places other than known cities and towns are expressions of the author's imagination or are used fictitiously. Any resemblance of these characters to actual persons, living in either the obstructed universe or the unobstructed universe, events or locales is purely coincidental.

Original painting and cover design - Loren Powell

ISBN O-9661065-1-2

Preface

HALF FACT AND HALF FICTION, this book is a response to the burgeoning interest in New Age publications and related coverage on TV, in magazines, newspapers, radio, and the internet. It provides an understanding of psychic experiences explained, e.g., in *The Unbstructed Universe*, published in 1940, reprinted in 1988. Fifty-five years of living according to the ideas set forth in such sources are reported by three principals, Bob, Tom, and Clair. Their dialogues are factual accounts of psychic experiences.

Their international reputations comprise an extraordinary 45-year record as university teachers and researchers in the fields of natural science, medical research, and the humanities. Collectively they've authored more than 20 non-fiction books, as well as several hundred articles published in scholarly journals, international dictionaries, and encyclopedias. Young scholars from various parts of the world have been guided by them to receive M.A., M.S., or Ph.D. degrees.

Chris, Pearl, and Eve, inventions of the writer, represent the curiosity and scepticism of the average reader. As their lives become entangled in the crush of daily living, gradual revelation of the spiritual development of Bob, Tom, and Clair, begun many years earlier, is an inspiration essential to resolving their problems.

Dedicated to the growing awareness of the one sure reality: *consciousness* - I AM, YOU ARE.

Chapter I

THE STRANGER SITTING next to me on the subway bench had been telling me some tall tales about Ouiji boards, apparitions, and more. I was so fascinated I had missed my train. Not that I believed them. I was losing patience and decided to cut him off short with a direct question.

I said, "Do you believe in ghosts?"

His smile looked like he was struggling to be patient. "Only those I've seen or talked with."

There was his train. I got to my feet and said, "Where'd you pick up stuff like that?"

"Not just I, " he said, "there are three of us."

He tipped his hat, the smile got even wider, and as he stepped into the train, he turned and added, "Next time we meet, I'll explain more fully."

The train doors closed, and I wondered how and when and even whether we'd meet again. My train arrived. On board I relaxed and unfolded the evening newspaper to learn what was happening in Boston. More delays on the damn tunnel.

I forgot about the stranger until nearly two months later. I had stopped in my favorite bar for a beer. He was on the stool next to me.

"Hi," he said, "how's progress on the tunnel?"

I probably blanched. Did he know - or only guess - the subject was dear to the heart of all Bostonians? He didn't sound like a Bostonian.

"You from Boston?"

The same smile, suggesting he knew more than I did. "I hail from other parts, but I've lived in Boston for some months. This is the worst city I've seen for traffic. They tell me the natives of Boston are already using abbreviations: BT and AT - Before the Tunnel, After the Tunnel."

"Oh . . . ."

His English was certainly not Bostonian. Not surprising, really. Most people these days don't sound like Bostonians. "Where from?"

"I move around a lot. Europe, Asia, Africa, Pacific Islands . . . the States, of course. I haven't yet learned much about South America."

"Uhuh." I was wondering what to talk about that would take as long as one draft beer, then a polite departure.

He looked at me intently. "Do you travel?"

"Abroad? Me? Oh, no! These 50 states give me more than one life time of travel. I doubt I'll ever have time to go abroad."

He was sipping a small straight-up drink. White . . . no, colorless. Gin? Vodka?

"What's your drink?" I asked.

"Quasi-absinth."

"Quasi . . . you mean anisette?"

"Right. I'm trying to get close to the spirit of Matisse and the other Impressionists.."

My beer was good for about three more swallows. This guy was off the wall. I took another fast gulp. "Last time we met," I was grasping for something to talk about, "you said there were three of you."

"Right. I'd been talking about simple facts in the psychic world. Beginners' information. You asked where I got that stuff, and I said there were three of us. Remember?"

"Oh, yes. Your train arrived. You promised to tell me more the next time we met." I took another swig of beer. "How'd you know we'd meet again?"

"It was a possibility."

2

"Uhuh." I had one swallow left; then a quick departure. "You come to this bar often?"

"My first time."

"You live near here?"

"It's on my way home."

"Okay . . . I guess I should ask. Where're your two buddies? The other two you mentioned?"

"We meet on Friday nights."

"You meet?" It was Friday. "What do you do when you meet?"

"Exchange experiences."

"You mean . . . the kinds of things you were talking about in the subway?"

"Oh, no . . . we left that behind long ago."

Well, my beer was gone. But I was getting curious to know just what this guy was talking about. I ordered another one.

When it came, I took a slow swallow and decided to come to the point. "You mean you left Ouiji boards and ghosts behind 'a long time ago'?"

He nodded.

I waited.

He ordered another anisette.

After his drink came, he stared at the back bar and began a recital that's still with me today. It was short. But it gave me a hell of a week, trying to figure out what it meant. And why it was something *I* should pay attention to. Why me? They're a lot of cukes around who'd appreciate it more, even though I doubt they'd understand what he was talking about.

He said there were valid "modes of discourse" beyond speech, and that more and more people were finding out how to prepare for the next phase. It wasn't quite clear to me what phase he was talking about. He said if I got interested, I could learn about all that later.

"Right now," he said, "Don't miss the chance to tune in on the new thought wave."

"Sorry," I said, "I've got no idea what you're talking about. What's the new thought wave?"

He looked at me for a moment, then sipped his second shot of anisette. His features were ordinary, sharp nose, a trifle long, mustache, blond hair, gray above his ears. His eyes were blue, a

3

deep blue that kept you looking longer than you should. I was getting used to his smile.

"The new thought wave is a new way to think about old thoughts."

I worked on my beer without comment, again trying to decide whether to down it quick and just leave.

He caught my eye. "Sorry you're tied up tonight."

Had I told him I was due at the Elks Club at 7:30? I didn't think so. Maybe he noticed when I glanced at my watch.

Without a pause he went on. "A session with the three of us might give you some clues. Maybe we'll meet again next Friday night."

He emptied the shot glass, dropped a ten-dollar bill on the counter, and headed for the door.

I sat there dumbfounded, thinking of this odd-ball meeting.. We meet twice in a tumultuous place like Boston. This time, accidentally in a bar he'd never been in before. Which was on his way home. He seemed to know about the Boston tunnel, but he wasn't a Bostonian. There were three of them who met every Friday night. They didn't talk about old fashioned stuff like Ouiji boards and apparitions. They just exchanged experiences.

"Hey, " I called after him, "where do you guys meet on Fridays?"

"The little Park just up the street. At seven - then we go on from there."

"Where do you go on to?" I asked. "What's your name?"

He was already out the door.

4

Chapter II

THAT BLUE-EYED GUY with the sharp nose was on my mind all of the next week. At odd moments, when I shoulda been paying attention to other things, I was framing questions I wanted to ask him and his buddies next Friday night. Then when I finally got to the Park, I was late. No blue-eyed guy, no buddies. And it was starting to rain.

I'm a male nurse. Sometimes I have to give shots and dole out the right pills. Nothing earth shaking, but you gotta keep your mind on what your doing. All week long I was disgusted how often that date at seven in the Park came to mind. I didn't make any mistakes, thinking about Friday . . . at least, I corrected them before it was serious - like counting pills again for good measure and finding my first count was wrong. I didn't make mistakes, but Friday night about five minutes to six, a patient gave me a problem that screwed up my time table.

Most of my long day on Friday I was too busy to think about anything but my job - and my date in the Park. I was supposed to get off at six. About five minutes to six this old man, late 70's, started complaining about stomach pains. He wanted to hang on to my wrist, so I stayed with him until we got hold of the Registered Nurse.. She put out a call for the Doc, who didn't get to us until 18 minutes to seven.

I gave the old man a pat on his shoulder, and said, "Okay my friend, you're in good hands now." But when I tried to leave his bedside, he grabbed my wrist again and held on tight.

The Doc saw it and nodded at me. "Better stay."

I stayed. And that's why I got to the Park 25 minutes late. No guy, no buddies, just a bunch of pigeons waiting for their regular post-dinner softies.

The rain was gentle, but it didn't help soothe my feathers. I'd forgot an umbrella in my haste to reach the Park. I wait the whole week, trot 14 blocks, and find nothing when I get there.

I thought about the Greek's for something to eat, but it didn't appeal to me. Chinese food? Italian? I decided on fish and chips at *Clam Chowder Charlie's*.

A half hour later, I'd finished eating the fish and chips, had a beer, and was beginning to feel better. The rain had stopped, and the light in the clouds showed me there was going to be a full moon peeking through any minute. Great night to walk home.

A few blocks later I passed the library. Library. I stopped and went back. Maybe the reference librarian could tell me where to look for answers to some of those questions I'd been straining to ask that trio of psychics.

She sent me to a section of the stacks called "Metaphysics" and 'New Age." I began running an eye over titles in this section: *The Betty Book, Our Unseen Guest, Unobstructed Universe, Life After Life, Saved by the Light, Celestine Prophesy* and many, many more.

I reached for one of them, *The Betty Book*, and began scanning pages. The overhead light in the stacks was dim, but I found myself getting fascinated with the writer's account of meeting a girl named Betty at a cocktail party. And right away, she sat opposite someone else at a Ouiji board, and the wooden pointer became so charged with energy, it flew off the board.

"They've got both the classics and recent popular ones."

I jumped. It was blue eyes! I held up the book. "You know this one?"

"Yes, and most of the others on those shelves."

I suddenly remembered the Park. "I came to the Park, but I was late. You had already gone."

"We usually only stay a few minutes . . . then move on to this place. They've got a seminar room they let us use on Friday nights."

"And you came to the stacks to get a book?"

"Now that I'm here, I'll take one back with me."

Later, I realized he hadn't really answered my question. At that moment, I had another one. "Would it be okay if I joined you and your friends? I'll keep quiet . . . while you 'exchange experiences.'"

"Sure. Maybe you'll think of a question or two."

Those that had bothered me all week suddenly became so entangled, I couldn't think of even one of them. I stalled for time. "Have you read this book?" I held up the one entitled *The Betty Book*.

"Yes, it's old, but a good one to start with. That and some others will prepare you for reading *The Unobstructed Universe*." He tapped the spine of the book on the book shelf. "It's also an old one. But I'm still trying to catch up with its deeper meanings."

Those blue eyes! I forced myself to look away. "What about the newer ones? Wouldn't it be better to read something up to date?"

The smile came back. "Some of the popular ones, those labeled 'New Age,' are fascinating accounts. Some are facts, some are fiction. But for substance read the older ones first. They'll give you a solid foundation for reading between the lines of New Age books."

He plucked *The Unobstructed Universe* from the shelf. "Come along, follow me to the seminar room."

I took *The Betty Book* with me, and remembered my library card had expired. They'd let me renew it. I looked at the section of the stacks we were leaving. I might want to come back.

The seminar room was small and quiet. There were only two tables and three lounge chairs. The overall lighting was bright enough to read in any part of the room.

An older man stood up and extended his hand. "I'm Bob. Tom's been telling me about you. I'm glad you found us."

I shook his hand, noted a firm grip that was a surprise at his age, and said, "I'm Christopher - Chris. Sorry I was late for the Park."

We sat in the three lounge chairs, and without thinking I began looking around the room for the third buddy. There was no one else in the room. "Tom, couldn't your other friend make it tonight?"

"Clair?" I saw him look at Bob. "She'll be along pretty soon."

I couldn't think of anything else to say, so I just sat still, expecting either Tom or Bob to begin exchanging experiences - whatever the hell they meant by that.

The older man, Bob, cleared his throat and glanced at Tom. There seemed to be some kind of unspoken understanding between them, because when Bob looked back at me, he said, "Would you feel comfortable exchanging experiences with us? I mean will you begin?"

Tom said, "Maybe you'll tell us what made you late at the Park."

Well, I'd been looking forward to this meeting for a week, but I sure didn't think for one minute that I'd be the first to offer an experience. I'd been asked, both men seem friendly and patient. So I told them about the old man and his stomach pains, about the nurse and the Doc. And then added, "Usually I'm through at six, so I would easily have been at the Park by seven."

Tom was smiling and nodding. "Why did you continue to stay with the patient after the nurse came?"

"He was hanging on to my wrist . . . I . . . well, it seemed to calm him down. So I decided to wait for the Doc."

Bob asked, "And after the Doc came?"

I was afraid one of them would ask that. "He saw the old man holding my wrist. The Doc asked me to stay."

Tom said, "Have you thought about why you did?"

I was getting uncomfortable. Who were these guys with all their questions! "No . . . I haven't thought about it."

"To please the Doc?" Bob's question came with a smile.

"I guess . . ."

Tom's eyes found mine. "What about the old man? Did you stay for him?"

"Of course!"

"Because you wanted to?"

"I guess . . . the old man needed me. I don't know how, but that contact holding my wrist . . ."

8

The pause was long. It began to be embarrassing.

Then Bob said, "He needed you more than the Doc. Was he okay when you left?"

Then I remembered what the Doc had said. "Chris, thanks for your help. Acute gastritis. The shot I gave him - and that grip he had on you . . . he's going to be okay."

I nodded at Bob and Tom. I hadn't told them what the Doc said, but they seemed to know anyhow.

The two men were very different to look at. The slim man with the graying blond hair and the sharp nose moved like a dancer. Slow, sure, beautifully balanced. I wondered what he did for a living. The older man was small, very erect, kinda professorial when he spoke. His words were measured, as though he might be tasting them on their way out. His crest of white hair was thin. He also had blue eyes, but they had a different look from Tom's. More patient, as though it could wait . . . whatever it was that had to wait. He didn't look like somebody's grandfather - too lively.

Tom's blue eyes almost talked for him. They seemed to be saying, "Out with it! Let's get on with it! Time's the essence!" And it appeared it didn't matter too much what it was the essence of, so long as we got on with it. But to contradict those eyes was a soft flow of elegant talk that soothed you, so you felt like taking all the time in the world. He was a little younger than Bob. I guess they were both old men - but when they talked or looked at you they seemed younger.

Bob crossed his legs, turned his proud-looking head away from us and said, "Not long ago, I had an NDE." His eyes came back to mine. "Near Death Experience."

I knew something about that kind of thing, working at the hospital. People who die - or seem to die, but don't - sometimes go through a way-out experience, literally way-out. Then come back to life to tell about it. The common report was about going down a tunnel toward a bright light.

Wanting to show I wasn't as dumb as they might think, I said, "You mean going down a tunnel toward a bright light?"

Bob uncrossed his legs and twisted around in his chair. "I'm a scientist," he said. "Work with powerful microscopes and study bugs. I'm especially interested in those that go through four stages from the beginning of life until they become bugs."

Wow, I thought. The guy's probably got a Ph.D., and I should address him as Dr. Bob. "University man?" I asked.

Tom nodded for him. "Bob spent nearly 40 years in a university lab. He's got five articles in *Men of Science* and another 100 in scholarly journals. He holds a number of patents." He seemed to be reading my mind when he added, "Everybody calls him Bob - no titles."

Bob straightened in his chair. "I'm concerned with metamorphosis, that is, the stages of development from the beginning stage of life to adult maturity. In this case, the metamorphosis of an insect from egg-to-adult."

Well, already I was impressed and waited to hear this man of science tell about his trip through a tunnel to find a bright light.

By now Bob was fidgeting in his chair. "That tunnel and light business, yes, a good many NDE's talk about a long tunnel leading to a bright light. My NDE was different. If I wanted to find a parallel I'd speak of the four stages of metamorphosis. My guide actually led me through four remarkable stages leading to the afterlife, a kind of spiritual metamorphosis. Am I communicating? Or has my scientific jargon obscured what I'm trying to say?"

I held up both hands. "Oh, no! I get it. You were guided through four . . . uh . . . progressive stages of getting where you were going." I caught his frown. "Where you were being led."

"To a *complete* metamorphosis, " he added. "Some are incomplete in the world of insects."

He was quiet for a moment, trying, I suspected to find simple ways of telling me about the four stages. Finally he said, "The first stage - like much of the living world - is the egg. Then comes the second stage, the larva, the worm, if you like. In the insect world the little worm eats and grows and eats and finally climbs up to the protective foliage of tree leaves, where the third stage becomes a cocoon or chrysalis. After a period of gestation, the cocoon opens and out flies a miraculous butterfly - the fourth stage."

He took a deep breath, looked over at Tom, and continued. "My guide walked me through the equivalent of these four stages in preparation and final realization of the afterlife."

I followed clearly what he was saying and wanted to ask about his guide, when Tom spoke up.

"Bob, Chris should hear about 'one step at a time.' Especially as someone who might get interested in New Age and old thought and all that implies."

"Right. Tell him about 'one step at a time.'"

If they heard my deep sigh, they didn't show it. I was getting a little nervous, because I was sure my presence was an interruption of their usual Friday meeting. Maybe they were just stalling until Clair arrived. I was also a little puzzled by the recital Bob had been making. At the hospital we were beginning to know something about these rare people who experience an NDE. What Bob had been talking about sounded more like a dream to me. At least if he died briefly, he hadn't said so.

Tom had a nice easy laugh. Even his eyes seemed to be smiling now. "This experience happened to me when I was 21. Yes, Chris, that long ago. I'd left my paternal home in the midwest at 17, spent time in Colorado, then back to the midwest, then off to California. Like most teenagers when I arrived, I joined the sun worshipers."

Bob cleared his throat, which I began to suspect was a habit. "Go on, Tom. Admit that you got as close to being a nudist as the public beach would allow."

That easy laugh. "Okay, Bob, you're right. My goal from early spring to late fall in southern California was to live on the beach and get the deepest tan possible. In those days only a few dermatologists were talking about the dangers of skin cancer."

I looked at him as a male nurse. "Tom, you bothered with skin cancer?"

"No . . . I've had a few warnings. But, no . . . I'm okay."

Bob cleared his throat again. "Get to the point, Tom . . . your experience on the beach."

"Well, I've always been an avid reader. I used to spend most of the day with dark glasses and a book, stretched out on a mat on the sand, baking in the sun. One late afternoon, when the sun had just dipped below the farthest edge of the sea, I heard someone behind me say in clear, strong voice: 'one step at a time.' I guess I had been dozing, and the voice woke me up."

Tom was still holding *The Unobstructed Universe* in his lap. He looked down at it for a moment, then continued. "I sat up slowly, not wanting to intrude on whoever was having a conversation behind me. I saw that the beach was practically

11

deserted. It was dinner time and all I could see ahead of me were sandpipers and sea gulls."

Bob cleared his throat again. "Tom, for a man of action, which you certainly are, it takes you a long time to get on with your experience."

"Okay, Bob, I'll come to the point. I twisted around slowly, again not wanting to intrude, because that strong voice had said again, even a little louder this time, 'one step at a time.' As far as I could twist comfortably to one side I saw nothing. Again the voice: 'one step at a time." I twisted to the other side, then turned fully around. The beach was empty. There was no one within four or five hundred yards. I looked again on all sides and one more time came the voice: 'one step at a time.'"

Well, I wasn't sure whether I was supposed to comment. Bob said nothing, just sat studying his hands.

Tom's smile was back. "Then I remembered the first time I heard that voice and that message." He paused and glanced at Bob, as though for confirmation. "It happened when I was six."

I don't know whether you've ever been caught in a situation like this one. I was wishing I'd never come into the damn library. But I was also sitting up very straight in my lounge chair now, waiting to hear what happened when he was six

He began again. "It was October. The midwestern temperature and freezing rain had created a kind of magic world for a six year old. I was sitting on the edge of our frozen lawn, staring up toward the corner street light. Between me and the light was a bare elm tree about 16 or 18 feet high, which had been planted several years earlier by my father. The naked limbs were coated with ice and, as the light came through them, seemed to form a circle. It was like looking at a magic crystal ball.[1]

"How long I had been staring, I don't know, but suddenly I felt two thumbs pressed into the little indentures at the back of my head, just above the neck. Gently they lifted me to my feet, and as I was being lifted I heard a clear strong voice say, 'You've got much to do, very much to do. But remember: one step at a time - take only one step at a time.' I began shivering. Not from the cold, but from some kind of inner charge of energy. Then my mother called me for supper."

---

[1]   Like the familiar ball used as a point of concentration.

Tom was staring off to one side, at a lamp sitting on a small table. "That phrase and the same strong voice returned when I was on the beach in Santa Monica at age 21. By then, I had already done a lot. Now, more than 50 years later, I can you assure there has been much more to do." A pause. "There's still more ahead."[2]

I opened my mouth to say something, then closed it, because the right words wouldn't come. The three of us sat silent for several minutes, then I remembered a question I had started to ask Bob, when Tom began his tale.

"Bob," I said, "That experience you were talking about, your NDE. I wanted to ask. Who was your guide? The one who took you through the four spiritual phases of metamorphosis?"

Bob looked at Tom, then back at me. "My guide was Clair."

---

[2] Betty White put it very simply: "Each individual is put into the world to do a job . . ." See further Stewart Edward White, *The Unobstructed Universe* (reprint), Ariel Press, Columbus, Ohio, 1988, p . 55; hereinafter referred to as: *The U.U.*

Chapter III

I WAS STANDING at the main counter of the library, showing the girl my expired card, my driver's license, and a credit card. It was the girl from the Reference Desk. She was chubby, bouncy when she moved, black eyes that flirted they way she used them. "You interested in this psychic business? We're gettin' a lotta customers for the New Age books. Not much for these old ones."

I was fascinated by the flirting eyes. Hell, one of these trips to the library I might make a date for dinner. "They tell me the old ones are good to begin with. You read this stuff?"

She laughed, and even a couple crooked front teeth didn't spoil that beautiful laugh. "Not me! But I'm a big reader - romance novels."

I waited. She was taking her time, and I was anxious to get back to those two old gentlemen left behind in another part of the library.

When she finished, I tucked the book under one arm and went to the seminar room. Bob wasn't back yet. He had suggested a short break for coffee, which was available near the entry to the library.

Tom looked up, as I dropped into the lounge chair. "Bob'll be back in a few minutes. I'll wait for him to tell you about Clair, except that she is his wife."

"Is?"

"Is? Oh . . . I understand your confusion. They were married a good many years ago, had a great life together - and in Bob's eyes and mine, they're still married. Only now they are in constant communication from two different planes."

I was carrying my paper cup of coffee. It seemed to me a good time to try it. After several sips of weak, tepid coffee, I said, "How? How do they communicate?"

"In various ways . . . we'll no doubt get into some of those ways, when Bob tells you about it."

The door opened, and Bob walked in with his coffee. "Have you two started without me?"

Tom grinned. "Not really. I just identified Clair as your wife, a very busy wife working on the other side."

I saw at once that Bob was pleased with the comment.

"They keep Clair busy, and she keeps us pretty busy. All three of us are still growing, learning, moving toward higher planes."

I forgot the coffee in my hand. "All three . . . growing, learning . . . ?"

Bob's look was patient. "Chris, we're starting you off with some involved, advanced thinking. Maybe it would be better if you have a question."

I had a question. "Your wife, Clair, does she see some of your old friends and relatives . . . I mean those on Clair's plane? Are they still the same? What are they doing? You said growing and learning. You mean even after going through that tunnel and seeing the light, there's still more to learn? What's Clair so busy doing?"

I realized I'd asked several questions. But frankly these guys were blowing my mind! People talking or communicating from two different planes. I wanted to hear more about that.

"Okay, Chris. One step at a time. First, there are a number of ways that communication is realized between the two planes. We'll talk about that presently. You wonder whether friends from this side who've joined Clair on that side have changed? What they're doing . . ." He raised his head a little. "I think Clair's here with us. She'll use my voice to speak to me and, at the same time, give you some answers."

I looked at Tom, hoping to see a reassuring nod. But his attention was totally on Bob.

Bob spoke, and his voice sounded the same. But the style of his speech had changed. "You ask if I see many of my old friends and relatives and, because there are so many of them, with new ones added, how do I sort them out? There is little need to answer the last part of your question, for you already know that my dimension is not bothered with time, space, and motion, which are obstructions to you. We use the essences of those so-called obstacles to advantage, which enables us to join those '50,000 angles that dance on the head of a pin,' leaving plenty of room for thousands more. You knew that when you accepted the essences of time as receptivity, space as conductivity, and motion as frequency, as was so beautifully described in the highly comprehensive book *The Unobstructed Universe.* "

I forced myself to cough, pulled out a handkerchief, and blew my nose. Tom noticed the interruption.

"You have a question Chris?"

It was an opening, but I didn't know how to use it to advantage. I managed to mumble, "I guess I've got to do some reading. Those are pretty big thoughts: time as receptivity, space as - " I felt helpless.

"Conductivity," Tom supplied.

I picked up at that point, "And motion as frequency. I don't pretend to understand it. But I guess I sorta sense the meaning."

Tom held a finger to his lips. I got the cue and waited for Bob, that is, Clair to continue.

"You also learned that those very essences are part of our life style; and does that also explain why I am but a thought away whenever you call for my attention? Do you remember when you thought nothing could surpass the speed of light? A mere snail's pace compared to the speed of thought; and that goes also for the head of a pin, which we might, for the occasion call 'The Conductivity Ball Room.'"

There was a long pause. I finally became aware I was sitting with my mouth open. It had dawned on me I was actually listening to *someone from the other side!*

Tom caught my distress. "Chris, Bob, let's talk about modes of communication. We've been using a very advanced technique. How about explaining the Ouiji board, Bob. You know a simple explanation to help Chris understand how it works. Okay?"

Bob's head was nodding. "Good idea. Change of pace." He looked down at his coffee. "Damn! I wish this was something stronger. It's really very weak."

We laughed, and I offered to run out for a bottle. Kidding, of course, but for a minute I thought the old man believed me.

"The Ouiji board," Bob started, "is probably best known as a parlor game. But most people don't know it's an American invention, not long before the beginning of World War I."

"Why?" I asked.

"Why was it invented? What were they trying to show or prove?" Bob shook his head. "There's been a lot of speculation. All we can be sure of is how it's used today. For some, it's not much more than a game at a party for two people to get better acquainted. Once in a while those two people sitting opposite one another produce charges of energy so strong that each accuses the other of pushing the pointer." He raised his eyebrows in a glance at me. "Ever try it?"

"Never . . . well, maybe once . . . at a party."

"And?"

"We thought it was boring."

"Well, if you read some of the early accounts of using a Ouiji board, you'll be impressed at the way that little three-legged planchette skips around on the board." Bob looked thoughtful for a minute. "Let me tell you about the first time Clair and I used it.

"When I suggested we try it, I know she was skeptical and did it just to please me. I explained about the printed alphabet at the top of the board, the words "yes" and "no," and numbers from one through nine and a zero. The sharp nose of the wooden planchette or pointer, spells out words, numbers, or simply answers 'yes' or 'no' to a question."

I thought it was time for a question. "Who decides who's going to push it to a number or a letter or 'yes'?"

Tom was smiling like a Cheshire cat. "Chris, no one decides who's pushing it. The energy generated by two people causes it to move."

"Any two people?"

Tom looked at Bob. "No . . . let me rephrase your question. 'Does it work better for some twosomes than others?' The answer would be yes. Some pairs at the Ouiji board - probably because of one of them - really make the pointer fly. If the attitude

18

is receptive and open-minded, any pair will do. But there's little doubt, some seem to have a much stronger receptivity than others. Bob, go on telling Chris about Clair's first try."

I was wondering whether this kind of receptivity was an example of Clair's explanation of time - unobstructed time.

"I had a son, 20 years old, when he died of Hodgkin's disease."

"When was that, Bob?"

"Quite a long time ago."

It didn't take a mind reader to see that Bob still felt the grief.

He was looking at the ceiling. His head came back, and his eyes found Tom's. "It was some months later, after bitter days and nights, that Clair and I were seated at the Ouiji board. The moment our two pairs of hands lightly touched the planchette it began to race all over the board.

"Clair was an absolute newcomer to this. She asked, 'Are you pushing it?' I assured her I wasn't and was equally sure she wasn't either. I asked her if she had a question.

"She shook her head. Then asked me, 'Do you?'

"I did. But I was almost afraid to ask it. At that time, I knew something about the psychic world, not much, but I had been aching to try to make contact with my son. Clair sensed what was on my mind. She spoke my son's name as a question. I nodded. All I wanted was some form of contact. Quickly the pointer began to swing back and forth from one letter to another, so fast, I stopped and asked her to write down what it was spelling. It was a poem."

Bob took a deep breath.

I knew it had happened a long time ago, and that the telling brought back the pain.

"This was the poem," he said.

> The earth is sodden by the tears
> of loved ones departed.
> Dry your tears, allay your fears,
> the spirit is newly restarted."

I looked at Tom, then back at Bob. What a beautiful way for a departed son to reassure his father that there was continuity.

No need for a father to worry about his son's well being, no need for his son to worry about a grieving father.

None of us spoke for several minutes. "Thanks Bob, Tom, for exchanging experiences. Can I come back next Friday?"

Chapter IV

ALL DAY MONDAY at the hospital I kept vacillating. Saturday and Sunday, after the new stuff thrown at me by Tom and Bob, I had felt dazed. I wanted to go out and tell all my friends about that night. But I didn't. They'd think I'd gone off my rocker. By Monday I was busting to talk with somebody about my new discoveries. But who?

About 3:30 in the afternoon, when I was having a coffee break, I bumped into Pearl waiting to use the machine. Pearl's the Registered Nurse who came to my rescue, when the old man was having stomach pains. I put a couple of quarters in the machine, placed a paper cup, and pressed the plunger.

As the cup was filling, I asked, "Cream, Pearl?"

She's about my age, in her forties, a little too plump from eating pizzas and heavy desserts. "Black, Chris . . . but I use three or four of those little packs of sugar."

I handed her the cup and watched her add so much sugar it made me cringe. "Pearl," I said, "you good for a ten-minute break?"

"That's what I'm on. You screwing up courage to ask me for a date?"

Pearl and I kid like that all the time. I guess I grinned, but I was thinking of something far more serious than a date. "Could we sneak outside with our coffee? Maybe in the rose garden leading to the parking garage."

21

I could see she was surprised.

"Why, Chris! I didn't know you cared! The rose garden!"

"Okay, gorgeous, have it your way. But I'd like to find a quiet place to talk. It's really important."

Her face suddenly looked sober. "Problem with one of the patients?"

"No, no . . . wait till we get outside."

In the rose garden I steered us to a concrete bench at one corner of the plot, as far away from the bordering sidewalk as possible. When we were seated, Pearl's crooked smile showed me she was getting curious.

She said, "You haven't got yourself in trouble with the administration, have you?"

The garden was empty, except for the two of us. "Pearl, you ever seen a patient who went through a Near Death Experience?"

"I dunno . . . maybe . . . why do you ask?"

It was hard for me to come right to the point. So I listened to myself stalling a bit. "Friday night," I said, "after I left the hospital, I headed for that Park about a mile north of here. I was late, so I ran to get there. It started to rain. When I got there, the people I was supposed to meet had left."

This wasn't the way I had planned to use our ten-minute break. So I tried another beginning.

"What's your opinion of people who claim they've had an NDE?"

"You throw those letters around like you were used to using them. What are you trying to tell me, Chris? Did you meet someone who had an NDE?"

"Sort of. Actually I think it was a dream"

"Now, Chris, nobody 'sort of' has a Near Death Experience. What are you trying to say? Have you been talking to some of those New Age readers?"

"Yes and no."

"Chris, you're awful vague. What's so serious you can't seem to get it out? This is your on-call girl friend." She planted both hands on her ample hips. "If I haven't seen it, it hasn't happened yet and probably never will. Spit it out. Have you seen a ghost or something?"

22

I looked her in the eye. "No, damn it, I haven't seen a ghost. I heard one talking."

She opened her mouth. Closed it. Then, "I think we better have a 20-minute break. Now what's this all about?"

How much could I tell Pearl?

"Did you ever hear of *The Betty Book*?"

She shook her head. "This book . . new one in New Age?"

"No . . . old one in the Old Age. Published a long time ago. It's about . . . well, they call them The Invisibles."

I'd spent the weekend reading and re-reading that book. This guy White, Steward Edward White, was the one who met Betty at the cocktail party. Later he and Betty tried the Ouiji board, and it started them off on a quest to discover the Other Side or whatever you want to call it. White was a Natural Scientist and writer. Hunted big game with Teddy Roosevelt. His training as a scientist kept their feet on the ground, while Betty was getting all kinds of messages - from somebody they called The Invisibles.

Pearl was reacting to my last words.

"You're talking about psychic communication, right?"

I nodded. "You know about that?"

She said nothing for a moment, then looked at me as though she was trying to figure something out. "I've heard of it. I even tried that Ouiji board at a friend's house one night. Not much happened. She said we didn't know how to concentrate. Then we tried to concentrate. Still nothing happened. She said maybe we were trying *too* hard to concentrate."

"Pearl, I met two gentlemen who've had some amazing experiences. They know so much about these things and have been at it so long, I have a hell of a time trying to follow what they're saying."

She put a hand over mine. "Chris, they're are a lot of strange people wandering around. Be careful."

I looked at the bush heavy with white roses just behind Pearl's head. It seemed to frame her brown hair like a halo. She sounded protective. "They're not like that, Pearl. No push. No hard sell. They're gentle. And they seem to know a lot that makes me want to know more."

"Did they tell you about some of the New Age psychics?"

It was getting harder to find the right way to tell Pearl how important they had become to me. I was beginning to think I

23

should have kept quiet. Telling somebody about it was sure different from experiencing it. Exchanging experiences. How could I make Pearl understand the difference?

"Pearl, do you like hand-woven woolens and silks and linen?"

She looked at me almost with alarm. "Hand-woven materials? Expensive. Yeah, I like them better than the machine-made stuff. Why'd you change the subject?"

"I haven't. Hold on a minute. Did you ever do any hand weaving?"

Pearl laughed. "I don't know a warp from woof - or do they call it a weft? Heddles, shafts . . . I heard a weaver talk about it once. They've got so many terms and gadgets and techniques I got lost. No, I've never tried it."

"They tell me a weaver enjoys the process as much as you enjoy the product."

"I could believe that, I guess. But what's that got to do with the New Age friends you were talking about?"

"Not exactly New Age . . . maybe they've got an Old Age understanding of the New Age."

"Okay, what's hand-weaving got to do with it?"

"Reading about NDE's and The Invisibles is like being fascinated with beautiful woven silk or linen - compared to hand-weaving the stuff yourself. You learn to know by doing, by making it so. Am I getting through to you?"

I felt a strange tremor shoot up my spine. I was watching Pearl's change of expression and, at the same time, listening to my words, as though somebody else was saying them through my voice.

She sat perfectly still and was silent so long I was afraid the spell was broken. For me it was a kind of spell. I kept thinking of my last words - the words that I spoke: ". . . learn to know by doing, by making it so."

Finally Pearl tossed her head, almost like somebody trying to throw something off, defiant, denying something.

"Chris . . . I had a friend . . . a close friend, who got wound up in all this psychic business. She started with the Ouiji board, then after a week or so, something called 'automatic writing.' That's when she told me about it."

Peal appeared a little calmer, now that she'd begun to talk. "She claimed that someone from the other side was guiding her pencil, writing messages that were the kind coming through on the Ouiji board. Only automatic writing was faster."

Now Pearl looked around the rose garden, as though making sure no one else was hearing her. "For a while, my friend seemed perfectly normal. Then I didn't see her for a few weeks. When I did, everything had changed."

Pearl looked at me, her eyes large and round. "She had gone from automatic writing to what she called 'direct voice.' Somebody else - from the other side - was speaking through her. One night I sat with her while she was on a couch in trance. And this voice started. It wasn't her voice - it was a *man's* voice!"

I'd forgot about coffee, and so had Pearl.

"You sure it was a man's voice?"

"Oh, yes! Deep, gruff . . . a macho man's voice."

I began to realize that I was the one doing the listening now. Pearl knew more about this than I did. "Did you understand what he - the voice - was saying?"

"For about two minutes. Then he switched to German. My friend doesn't know any foreign languages. And I don't know much German . . . just enough to recognize it when I hear it."

She sighed, hesitated. "Chris, I'm not trying to scare you, but my friend went farther than that. She began to make contact with the other side - at least she claimed she did - without any Ouiji board or automatic writing or direct voice. Now she just called it 'direct.' Everything came to her, in her mind, *direct.*"

"How did that work?"

"Without writing or strange voices these thoughts came directly into her head. She told me some of them."

"When these thoughts came direct, was she in trance?"

"No. And that scared me."

"How?"

"Well, she had told me they weren't *her* thoughts. They were thoughts from the other side. They begin to sound like a world I didn't know. Not my friend's world. *Their* world."

Well, I sat there getting a little scared myself, listening to Pearl talk and seeing her so troubled. I thought I'd say something to calm her down. "That sounds pretty far out. But at least your friend wasn't harmed, was she?"

Pearl discovered her coffee again and took a big gulp. She looked at me. "Chris, she had to undergo treatment from a psychiatrist . . . for nearly a year. She never talks about it any more."

"Never?"

"Not a word." She looked at me with fear in her eyes. "Be careful, Chris. Stay away from it. It's dangerous!"

Now human beings are likely to be a bit unpredictable. Instead of accepting her warning, instead of backing off, you know what? I could only think, *now* I've got an experience to exchange with Tom and Bob . . . and Clair."

Chapter V

THE FOLLOWING FRIDAY, I arrived at the Park about 10 minutes to seven. It was mid-May, no rain, and daylight saving made it early twilight. Those pigeons were waddling around like they owned the place, waiting for somebody to throw them some crumbs. I'd gone to *Clam Chowder Charlie's* for a quick bite and stuffed my pockets with soda crackers. I didn't tease those pigeons, but I fed them slowly, so I could make friends. The more I fed them the friendlier they got. Those birds were so friendly I nearly forgot Tom and Bob, until I heard Tom's smooth voice coming up behind me.

"Hi, Chris. Right on time."

I turned. "Hello, Tom." I looked around for Bob. "Is Bob late?"

"No," he pointed, "he's over there talking to that small dogwood tree."

"He's *what*?"

"He frequently talks to plants and animals. That's why we meet here in the Park for a few minutes before going on to the library."

"To talk to plants and animals?"

"Bob does. I watch him and listen." He paused. "That's not so strange, Chris . . . in fact, it's pretty close to what you were doing a moment ago feeding pigeons. There are more direct ways of making contact than using speech."

27

He waved a hand at the expanse of the Park. "This wonderful green space, with these lively forms of nature, reminds us that we're all takers and givers of energy. It sets the mood for our exchange of experiences in the seminar room."

Bob came up with his dignified walk and erect set of his head. "Evening, Chris. Beautiful kinds of life in this place. That small tree over there has paid attention to my chatter this spring. It has put out leaves and blossoms in abundance."

I wanted to ask him what he and the tree had been talking about. But wisely I kept my thoughts to myself. Talking to a dogwood tree! Otherwise, Bob seemed perfectly sane.

He and Tom exchanged glances, nodded, and the three of us started walking toward the library. A thought struck me.

"Bob, do you gentlemen come here to the Park in the winter, even if it snows?"

"Oh, yes. Some forms of life are in hibernation, but others are struggling to make it through the winter. They, too, are quiescent."

"How does snow help?"

"I'm not speaking of the little creatures in hibernation. They've stored some food, but eat very little. They're relatively inactive. But plant life is different in the winter. Dry cold creates the need for moisture, precisely what the plants are waiting for when it snows."

In a few minutes, we were in the library. They both nodded to the two girl librarians smiling from behind the checkout counter. I noticed my black-eyed girl at the Reference Desk, some distance away, and made sure she saw my greeting. The smile I got back looked encouraging.

Back in the seminar room Tom said, "Chris, you started us off last week. Would you like to do it again?"

I rested both my arms on the chair arms, crossed my legs, and looked at Tom and then Bob. "Sure. Why not." I was dying to tell them about my talk with Pearl to hear what they'd say about the friend who got in trouble.

In great detail I told them everything Pearl and I had talked about. Except I didn't mention my remark about Bob's NDE being a dream. When they heard about the friend being under psychiatric care for nearly a year, I saw them exchange knowing looks.

Tom was the first to speak. "Your friend Pearl gave you a good account of some basic modes of communication. There are

28

more ways than those she mentioned for making contact with the other side. Eventually we'll talk about them too. Right now, you're worried that Pearl's friend got in trouble." He arched an eye toward Bob. "Remember the reminder I received several times? One step at a time. Pearl's friend was trying to move too fast."

"What happens, when you move too fast?"

"Pranksters," Bob said.

"Pranksters? You mean people . . . spirits on the other side playing tricks?"

Tom's smile had disappeared. "Something like that. An old bromide we learned from the author of *The Betty Book* you are reading prevents that kind of interference. Mr. White told me - "

"You knew him, the famous Stewart Edward White?"

"Only during one summer - at Laguna Beach in California. Mr. White said," Tom continued, "'if you fill your mind full of positive thoughts, absolutely full, so there's no room for even one negative thought, you can avoid the pranksters.'"

I listened to what he was saying, not quite sure how to keep my mind filled with positive thoughts. I decided to ask. "How do you do that? Keep your mind filled with positive thoughts?"

"It takes practice. The more you do it the easier it becomes. Your question makes me think about Mr. White's recipe for meditating."

"He had a recipe for meditation?"

"That's my word for it. His approach was developed by trial and error. He tried a method practiced by some people. Lie down in a supine position and concentrate on each muscle - feet, legs, arms, abdomen - to relax. Mr. White said the more he tried to get each set of muscles to relax the more tense he became. So he devised a different approach. And for him it worked. It works for me, too. Not just for meditation but also in another application."

"Tell me."

"He said that after lying down for a few minutes he attached his attention and mind on little incidental sounds - a water faucet dripping in another room, the undifferentiated hum of traffic outside, the distant mingle of voices from a nearby children's playground. He explained that by letting his mind register those small distractions, which required no thought of particular concentration, it freed the larger portion of his mind to be alert for other things. It made him keenly receptive."

I thought about that for a moment. "Is that filling your mind with positive thoughts?"

"No, but it makes you receptive to them. Mr. White said that at the beginning of meditation he used to repeat to himself a little phrase: 'Only the positive may enter; none others need apply.'"

"And it worked?"

"He never needed psychiatric help."

I was thinking that guy White must have been a real inspiration to know. "Had you been involved with this stuff very long when you met him?"

"Six or eight months, I suppose. But I'd read all the Betty books - there are several more than the one you have - including *The Unobstructed Universe*."

"Did you see him again, after that summer?"

"No, a few months later I was called up for military service in World War II."

Something told me not to press any farther. But I was beginning to have a lot of questions. "You said Mr. White's recipe for meditation works for something else. What?"

"I found I could use it to achieve a kind of super-attentive perception." Tom frowned, as though he might be trying to find the right words. "I found that if I went through the same steps of listening for inconsequential sounds, which required nothing of my mind except being aware of their presence, it freed the mind for other things. For example, it became a habit when I attended an important lecture or sat in on a committee or faculty meeting at the University. I could absorb and recall everything discussed with unusual clarity. It worked the first time I tried it, so I began to develop it." He grinned like a boy caught with his hand in the cookie jar. "By now it's been a habit for many years. Try it sometime, Chris. See if it works."

Bob was squirming in his chair. I knew he had something on his mind. "I've tried it, Chris. Works for meditation without fail. But the way Tom uses it . . . for me it doesn't seem to work."

I was afraid we'd loose our subject, which was my concern about Pearl's friend. "Professor," I said to Bob, "Can you tell me a little more about those 'one-at-a-time steps' in learning ways to communicate with the other side?"

Bob straightened up in his lounge chair slightly and, when he spoke, reminded me of an old prof of mine in med school. "The progression from Ouiji board to automatic writing can be quite rapid. After all, they're both forms of spelling out words. And, of course, the pointer is slower than the pen. One is a natural extension of the other." He paused. "Direct voice is a different matter."

Tom was nodding. "It's important for Chris to know about it. Chris, you are interested in the things we're exploring, no?"

I really hadn't thought about it. But, of course, he was right. I *was* getting more enthusiastic the more I heard.

"Bob's point is a good one. The progression from Ouiji board to automatic writing is easy to make and need not be considered moving too fast. In a sense the two are actually 'one-and-the-same step at a time.'"

He stood up and walked to a stack of drawers, the kind that house maps. He produced a key for one of these, slid out a drawer, and removed a Ouiji board and planchette.

"They let me use this drawer. Why don't we give you a start? You and Bob."

Well, without thinking of Pearl's friend, I stood up and walked to one of the tables. Tom placed the board so that it was diagonal to the end chair and first side chair. Bob was already sitting down in the end chair.

His finger tips rested lightly on the broad end of the little planchette. When he nodded for me to place my hands just beyond his, I sat down facing him and tried to imitate the position of his hands. For several moments I was disappointed. I couldn't feel a thing.

Then I saw Bob close his eyes. I followed his lead. Suddenly that pointer came to life. It darted up to the alphabet, then down to "yes," then back to the alphabet and at a slower pace began to stop at different letters.

Tom had a pencil at the ready. The pointer spelled out a message, which he read to us:

DO YOU HAVE A QUESTION

Bob looked at me, I looked at him, then Tom. Damn! I had so many questions in my head, but I couldn't think of how to ask one of them! Finally I blurted out: "Who is this? Who are you?"

The pointer raced back and forth among the letters of the alphabet at a pace so fast, Tom had trouble keeping up with it. When it stopped moving, Tom read:

A FRIEND OF YOURS WE TALKED LAST WEEK HAVE YOU FORGOTTEN ALREADY

I didn't know what to say. I had been talking with a spirit last week? No way! This must be one of those pranksters they told me about.

Again the planchette was flying among the letters of the alphabet. When Tom read it back, the message was:

PERHAPS YOU TOOK MY WORDS TOO LITERALLY I WAS TALKING TO YOU THROUGH BOB NOW DO YOU REMEMBER

"Clair!" we all said at the same time.

I was dumbfounded, at first. Then it dawned on me. The first time I heard from Clair, it was through Bob's voice. This time the message came through without any misspelling or hesitation on a Ouiji board - but it was Bob's doing, this time sitting opposite me at a Ouiji board.

"Bob" I said in a low quiet voice, "you sure you aren't pushing the pointer?"

Before I had finished speaking the pointer was whirling from one letter to another. This time, when Tom read it back, I felt foolish.

CHRIS YOU FAILED TO MENTION THAT WHEN YOU WERE TALKING WITH PEARL YOU SAID BOBS NDE WAS ACTUALLY A DREAM

I was probably blushing. Gee, I didn't know what to say. I couldn't look Bob or Tom in the face. Neither of them could have known that. Bob couldn't be pushing the planchette.

Once again the pointer was moving. Now it was more deliberate, as though to emphasize the message. Tom read it to us when the planchette stopped:

DO NOT BE EMBARRASSED THE NDE IS CROSSING OVER TO THIS SIDE AND A REVIEW OF YOUR LIFE IT CAN ALSO BE REVEALED IN A DREAM LIKE THE FOUR STAGES OF METAMORPHOSIS BOB CAN EXPLAIN GOODNIGHT TO THE THREE OF YOU

Without a word Bob got up and went back to his lounge chair. Tom picked up the board and pointer and returned them to the drawer. I left the table and sat down again in the easy chair.

When Tom found his seat, Bob spoke.

32

"Chris, it's not uncommon to hear of someone experiencing an NDE in a different form. Two things are essential. One, an understanding of the stages passed through to the other side. In my case, a guide, Clair, talked me through the same thing in a dream in the form of the four stages of a complete metamorphosis. Nothing could be more vivid. The second essential thing of an NDE, which I have yet to experience, is the life review."

Bob was nodding. " I thanked Clair for the most amazing revelation of my life. And when I did, I got the strong tingling sensation over my whole body, which is my sure sign that my message has been received."

Tom said, "Get Dannion Brinkley's two books to read a variety of accounts of persons who've experienced an NDE. Brinkley has been recognized as one of the most gifted psychics by Raymond Moody, M.D. and Ph.D., who wrote *Life After Life*. Brinkley had an NDE *twice*. You might read all three of these New Age books."[1]

I wrote down the names and suggested a coffee break.

---

[1] For an extensive account of many different kinds of NDE's see further Jean Ritchie, *Death's Door*, Dell Publishing, New York City, 1996, 279pp.

Chapter VI

ON THE COFFEE BREAK I tried to find the Reference Librarian, but she had gone off somewhere on her own coffee break. So I followed Tom and Bob back to the seminar room.

Inside I said, "Bob, I got one big question. What's this thing about talking to dogwood trees and other things in the Park? Do they talk back?"

Bob had found his favorite lounge chair. "Not exactly talk back. But we manage to communicate."

By now I was getting used to his roundabout manner of speech. "Meaning? Bob, excuse me for being so direct. But sometimes, you leave me in the dark. Just what are you saying?"

Tom spoke up quickly. "Chris, you have to understand that when you know as much as Professor Bob," (I'd not yet heard him be so formal) "it takes him a while to simplify his dialogue to our level of understanding."

Well, that response chopped me down to size. Who was I, a male nurse working for only two bucks above the minimum wage, to be asking Professor Bob to speak so I could understand him. I decided to be quiet and see what developed.

"Plants and animals are alive, filled with energy, and, like you and me, are growing toward something. The ultimate objective, at this point, is unimportant, but they're growing and developing in the same flow of energy that we depend on. They're just occupying a different phase."

Tom took over. "Chris, my grandfather - maternal grandfather - could speak to animals. It was common knowledge in the small town where he lived in the midwest that he managed to communicate with wild squirrels, rabbits, all kinds of birds - even a fox - and feed them out of his hand, except for the fox. Remembering that, I tried to talk to deer in a retreat in the hills of West Virginia. After a few days, the deer would listen to me, stamp their feet, toss their heads, wait until I had more to say, then saunter off when I had run out of things to talk about. I don't ask you to believe this, Chris, but after a couple of weeks, I really think they understood what I was trying to tell them. And I remembered my grandfather."

"And Bob talks to plants in the Park." I turned to Bob. "Can you tell me more about that?"

"Chris, some people can talk to plants and affect their growth. They've made experiments with music and found that some kinds will encourage growth and other kinds hold back normal growth. And one more for the record book. Experiments are ongoing to show that plants can communicate with each other."

Now look. I'm a male nurse. One thing you learn real quick in a job like that is who's honest and who's faking. I needed more information. "Bob, I'm slow getting your meaning sometimes. You say, some people can make plants grow, just by talking to them. Is that what you said?"

"Yes, that's what I said. Interest started about 25 or 30 years ago, at first with a few hardy experimenters. By now a lot of young plant physiologists have shown positive results that have removed any doubt."

"Plant physiologists. Guess that's why I never heard of it in the hospital." The old professor was so stuffed with information I was almost afraid to ask more questions.

Tom spoke up. "Some years ago Bob was in touch with Dr. J. B. Rhine at Duke University."

"Rhine?"

"He's the one who founded the Department of Parapsychology at Duke. A lot of work with ESP - Extra Sensory Perception. Much published on that subject with positive results. But, Bob, I was thinking of the summer he sent his assistant out to see us, remember?"

"Very well. He wanted to consult with our plant pathologist at the University. Dr. Rhine was interested in ongoing experiments with the effect of mental concentration on plant growth."

"University project?"

"Dr. Rhine had his assistant put seeds on graph paper, circle some of them, then close it off with a moist blotter cover. He put this in the trunk of his car, and when driving to and from the University he concentrated on growth. After ten days or so, he opened it up and found the circled seeds had developed a larger root growth than those not circled. To be as scientifically accurate as possible, he reversed the process. On a new batch he concentrated on the seeds not circled. This time, they were the ones with greater growth."

"Why did he do it twice?"

"Some critic said maybe there was something in the ink used to circle the first group of seeds. So they tried the opposite to satisfy the critic." Bob thought minute. "As Rhine's assistant explained it to me, the original concept was to influence germination through prayer with direct positive thought, thus eliminating religious interpretations. Objectivity was attained through positive thought alone, not necessarily through prayer. The experiment was intended to prove that plant life is closely attuned to all elements of nature."

"What did Dr. Rhine want with your plant pathologist?"

"My colleague was a world authority on tomato gall. The closest thing to cancer in the plant world. Dr. Rhine was interested in possible applications of the power of thought to affect human cancer."

Tom said, "That was a stimulating summer. We had a theoretical mathematician and a physicist from Columbia University."

"And a painter and a musician," Bob added.

"All of us open-minded," Tom said. "We learned a lot."

"About treating cancer?"

"No, I don't know the final result of that experiment. But I was especially interested in things the physicist said. He told us that one wall of his office was covered with electrical switches. He had installed one of those tall library ladders that move on rollers along the wall. The physicist said he spent time throwing switches at random to see their effect."

"Effect on what?"

Tom laughed. "Chris, my knowledge of physics is no greater than yours. I got lost in his explanation. But the significant point, Bob and I agreed later, was the physicist's use of random and chance as a procedure."

"And most scientists don't believe in random and chance, that it?"

"More than that, Chris. They're bound to Galileo and reproducible experiments."

Bob spoke up. "White wrote that they hadn't yet learned 'to work in the nature of the substance.' He meant that their closed minds to psychic experiments blocked any chance of success."

This was getting over my head. But I still wanted to know about music having an affect on plants. "Bob, what about music and plants? That sounds pretty far out."

Tom spoke up again. "I can help with that question. My field is music, all kinds of music, anywhere in the world."

Music of the whole world . . . ? I waited for him to go on.

"Not long ago under laboratory conditions they conducted an experiment by playing Western art music - Mozart, Bach, Beethoven - for a group of plants. Remarkably the music-listening plants actually *leaned toward the speakers* in their growth."

He told me about a major magazine that published an article on the subject along with pictures."Tom, you said classical music -"

"Correction. I said art music. Classical, Baroque, Romantic - these are some of the kinds of art music."

These guys were damned precise in what they said and even picky about what you said. "Okay, art music. What about other kinds of music? Like acid rock?"

"When they used rock music the plants leaned away from the speakers. Maybe it was the presence of too much energy in the high partials - the overtones. Maybe too many decibels - too loud. Read about it for yourself. If you have trouble finding it, I'll lend you my copy."

By now I was beginning to understand why Friday night meetings started in the Park. But Bob had said one more thing that I really couldn't believe. Plants can communicate with other plants. "Bob," I said, "one more question. You said plants can communicate with other plants. Will you explain how you know that?"

Bob was smiling patiently, I realized, as though trying to use words a 6th grader would understand. "Sure, Chris, I'll gladly explain how we know they can communicate. I'll give you an example. Some trees have life-threatening natural enemies, like bark beetles and pine bores. When a pest like that attacks a tree, the flow of sap increases, so that the sticky substance surrounds the invader, traps him, mires him down so he can't move. If the sap flow is sufficient, the tree can defend itself, if not, it will probably die."

"I understand, Bob, but that's not an example of communication between plants."

"Right, Chris. The example is necessary for you to understand our evidence of plant communication."

He was warming to his subject. I waited.

"This phenomenon has occupied the special interest of some botanists. They are finding that when a tree is affected by an attack of beetles causing the responding increase in sap flow, sometimes the sap flow of other trees surrounding it - trees *not* under attack by the beetles - also increases, as though defending the tree from invasion."

"How does the damaged tree let the other trees know about it? *How* does it communicate?"

"They don't yet know. The scientists are trying to figure it out."

All the information about talking to plants and animals, plants talking to plants, music affecting plants . . . at this point it was not at all clear where the facts were leading me. But it was beginning to look likely that all these things were connected with something big and with one another.

Chapter VII

THE NEXT DAY, after a sleepless night thinking of the session with Bob, Tom, and Clair, I was even more wound up and had to talk to somebody about what had happened to me. So, I phoned Pearl. Neither of us had to work that Saturday. I ask if she was brave enough to sample my new recipe for scallops. She said scallops made her break out in a rash. So, we ended up at *Clam Chowder Charlie's*, which has great food at good prices.

Back at the two very small rooms I rent (Boston rents are over the moon!} we had some frozen Key lime pie as dessert. I watched her put away two or three bites and then came to the point.

"Pearl, about your friend who got in trouble - "

"You still fooling around with those new buddies of yours? Now I know why I got invited for scallops."

"Now, Pearl, that's part of the reason. I did talk to them again last night - and I thought you'd be interested in what I learned." I finished my beer, which tasted kinda strange with the Key Lime pie. "Besides, I just wanted to see you again - away from the sweat shop."

If she believed what I said, I couldn't tell. She shrugged, but didn't smile.

"I'd like you to meet these people sometime. I know you'd be impressed."

"People? How many?"

"Three . . . well, actually two . . . three if you count the one I said I didn't see but talked with."

She gave me a look. "The ghost. You mean number three is the ghost."

This conversation wasn't going the way I had planned. Here we were, off on the wrong foot. I thought a change of subject might help. "Have another piece of pie, Pearl." I got up from the table. "Be right back. I want to show you something I bought this morning at a book store."

"You buying books? I didn't know you were much of a reader."

I called back to her as I went to the bedroom and pulled a Ouiji board out from under the bed. "Yeah, I bought a book. But something else, too." As I came back I held up the board in one hand and the pointer in the other. "You ever made one of these work?"

The look on Pearl's face was not encouraging. In fact, she didn't even answer.

I put the board between us on the table.

"Look, Chris, I'm not interested. I thought you'd be bright enough to get that from what I told you in the rose garden."

Without looking at her I put the pointer on the board and dropped my fingers on it. Then I looked up. "This sure won't work, if you don't help."

For a full minute she glared at me. Then gradually I saw the corners of her lips turn up into a faint smile. "Chris, you're a dog!" She put her fingers on the pointer.

Well, we sat there two or three minutes. Nothing happened. Her smile had disappeared. I felt stupid as hell. What was I supposed to do now? What was it Tom talked about? What did he say that writer White did to meditate?

I took my hands off the pointer. Pearl did the same. "I'd like you to try something, Pearl. Can you hear that rumble and hum of the traffic outside?"

She looked surprised. "Sure . . . so?"

"And can you hear that noisy neon tube humming from the kitchenette? The one I rigged up as a shop light?"

"Of course."

I could see she was really listening now. "And the clucking little noise from the leaking toilet? I forgot to shut the bathroom door."

"You think I've got ear problems? I hear it. I hear all three of those sounds."

I put my fingers back on the pointer.

"Good. Now just go on listening to those three sounds. Nothing else. Don't think about anything we've been discussing. Just concentrate on those three little sounds."

I watched her closely. She wasn't looking at me but stared unfocused past the bedroom door. Slowly her hands went back to the pointer, opposite mine.

Pearl gave a big, deep sigh. And suddenly the pointer began sliding back and forth between the letters of the alphabet.

"Keep listening to the sounds," I said.

She did. I tried to memorize the letters and what was being spelled out. I had trouble keeping up with it. Then it hesitated, quivered, and stopped.

Pearl looked at me. Surprise, alarm, disbelief on her face.

"Chris, I know you want this thing to work. But really, you shouldn't push it around like that."

I grinned. "You took those words out of my mouth. I was about to ask, 'are you pushing it?'"

I got up and went to an end table where I kept a note pad and pencil. I wrote slowly in capital letters without punctuation:

PEARL YOU DIDNT TELL CHRIS HER FRIEND IS YOUR SISTER

When I showed it to Pearl, I don't know who was more surprised. When the full jolt hit her, she clapped a hand to her mouth.

I said softly, "Jeez, Pearl, I sure didn't know your friend who got in trouble was your sister. She okay now?"

Pearl was staring at the capital letters and shaking her head.

We put the board away after that, talked a little bit about patients at the hospital, and a half hour later I walked Pearl home. Would you believe it? We met at my place three times during the next week, trying the Ouiji board, always starting off listening for little sounds that didn't require any thinking.

Before the next Friday night, I finished reading *The Betty Book* and tried my hand at automatic writing.

43

Chapter VIII

WHEN FRIDAY CAME, we got a messy emergency at the hospital. Every extra hand was needed, including male nurses. A three-car smash-up, one of them a bus loaded with kids in the first six grades of grammar school. There were five DOA's, when the ambulances began arriving, around 5:30. Three were children, one was the driver of one of the cars, the other was the bus driver. The driver of the third car and 14 children were alive but critically injured. Along with everybody available that afternoon I worked so hard, so fast, and prayed so much that by the time I could take a shower and change, I was almost a basket case myself. The smell of death, antiseptics, mangled limbs, and bloody, bloody bodies was still in my nose, when I got out of a long shower taken with a lot of soap.

I looked at my watch: 7:40. No supper, no Park, a quick run to the library? Remembering all the questions that had been building up during the week I raced for the door and decided to try the pacing I learned as a Boy Scout, 50 paces running alternately with 50 paces walking fast to reach the library. I made it in 11 minutes. Tom and Bob were in the seminar room. They looked up when I entered.

"Little crisis at the hospital?"

"Big one," I said and dropped into a lounge chair.

Tom seemed to know I'd been running. So instead of waiting for me to explain he said, "Bob was getting a kind of

45

scolding from Clair. She does that now and then, when she gets impatient with what she often reminds us are the obstacles of our obstructed universe. Tempered, of course, with a reminder that the universe has two halves, one obstructed, one unobstructed." He looked at Bob, who was holding a pen, and obviously had been writing something. "The matter on Bob's mind was so complicated, that he thought it might be wise to go back to the slow method of communication, automatic writing."

I watched with fascination as Bob's pen began moving rapidly. I got up and looked over his shoulder. The message from Clair read: "Words you are presently writing are from more than a single source. Like you, I must gather information from a higher authority on occasions such as this. By now you know the procedure. I need not elaborate."[1]

I looked from one to the other, waiting for one of them to explain. They didn't. Bob put his pen away and returned to his lounge chair. Puzzled I said, "I didn't mean to interrupt. Go on with whatever you were doing."

"I've finished," he said. "The question in my mind had to do with dogs. It got complicated, so I asked Clair to explain. She did so, very simply. She referred to something Betty White said - from the other side - a long time ago, when Stewart Edward White asked about their dogs. They had died, and Stewart wondered whether they were part of this crossing over to the other side. Clair simply quoted Stewart when he asked Betty: 'How about dogs? Have you got dogs in your world?' 'Of course I have my dogs; and I love them.' Then 'They continue on individually as you do? As dogs I mean.' 'The individual is immortal.'[2]

"Clair went on to say, 'Their progression to this side is no different from ours.'"

I looked at Tom for help. He said nothing. How could these two wise old men be talking about dogs! I guess Bob read my mind, something I found out later he could do on occasion.

"You might be wondering, Chris, why we're interested in dogs. Unfortunately, if some have had NDEs - and they probably have - we haven't learned enough of their language to find out."

I gulped and waited.

---

[1] cf. *The U.U.*, p. 224.
[2] see further op. cit., *passim*.

Bob went on. "The other day, during a break in our rainy Boston weather, I took a walk down one of our native tree-lined streets. The air was fresh, and I felt good. It reminded me of many joyful walks I used to take through the woods surrounding our place in the Catskills, always with one of our dogs. Our first dog was a Siberian Husky, named 'Kiska.' After she died, we acquired another pup, an Alaskan Malamout. We named her 'Tadluk.' Which means Little Snow-Shoe, in Aleut. Those dogs, similar in appearance, were my constant companions.

"I missed them terribly, when each passed on. Thinking about the dogs as I walked alone, wishing I had Tadluk for company, the thought occurred to me that she was very much alive in her own universe. Betty White, from the other side, often spoke of her dogs. It suddenly occurred to me that Tadluk, 'Ook' for short, may be wondering why I don't call her anymore. And then I remembered an article read recently about how dogs think. A photo showed a large boxer with an expression of great anticipation. The caption read: 'Eagerly awaiting for his master to say: "Let's go for a walk."'

"With that picture in mind I thought, why not call Tadluk and ask her to join me. Mentally I practically yelled: 'Ook, let's go for a walk.' Believe me when I say I was overwhelmed by a huge tingle or shock wave - so vivid that I actually stepped aside to keep from being bowled over. That dog was all over me, and I shared her excitement. Suddenly I visualized the expectant look on the photo of the boxer and gave the same strong mental call: 'Kiska, come on girl, join us!'

"I experienced exactly the same 'blast' I had got with Tadluk's presence. Those dogs were so real I could almost hear their howls of pleasure; and I wept at the reunion. The Malamut is first cousin to the wolf. I had often talked to Ook about such matters as her howl. This was serious stuff. There was meaning in her howl. I talked to her to see if she would respond. There were some muted sounds, and during the discussion she looked straight into my eyes, as though to say, 'the howl is a private matter!' With a little prompting she responded in the only way she could, opening up with such intensity, reaching sounds higher than ever before. The howl to end all howls. The sincerity of her attempt to communicate was noted. At the end of the demonstration she did not wag her tail, lick my face, or offer any other acts of enthusiasm.

She gave me a final stare, turned, and walked away with dignity. Normally she was a lovable companion, whenever we went out for a walk. She would howl in sheer joy at my company. Well, I had probably overstepped our relationship in the past, when I coaxed her to howl - when it wasn't volunteered. It was in moments like those that I saw the wolf in her makeup.

"I wept with a tightness in my throat all the way home, enough so that my wife asked why my eyes were red. I lied. 'That cold, brisk wind in my face drew tears.'"

Bob looked at me. "Of course, by now, Clair knows all about it. When you came in, I was trying to learn a little more about the dogdom part of the unobstructed universe." He swallowed hard. "If we can call for a reunion with our dogs, why not our friends and relatives, who also feel forgotten."

I sat wondering what to say. Here I run-walk as fast as possible on a Friday night after one hell of a night in emergency to hear about the after-life of dogs. Well, I respected these guys. But, damn! who cares that much about dogs! Then, when I thought about it, obviously Bob did. I had to think some more about friends and relatives.

I felt brave, so I asked, "Bob, can you tell me something about Clair? I mean who she is . . . or was? I mean on this side?"

My fooling around with Pearl on the Ouiji board seemed like beginner's stuff - which, of course, it was.

"Clair?"

I could see Bob making an effort to come back from wherever he was.

"Clair has a no-nonsense, witty attitude that sometimes touches sarcasm, especially when it is intended to drive home a needless point. She makes us realize that thoughtless questions deserve mocking answers. As a case in point: once I asked a foolish question - which I've forgot by now - realized I shouldn't have asked it and attempted to cover by adding: 'Sorry, I shouldn't have asked, it's probably a waste of your time.' The answer to my question came back at once, compounding the reason it shouldn't have been asked in the first place. 'Again you are obstructed by time. How can you waste *my* time? I have eternity. It's *you* who are wasting your own time, which should be put to better use.'

"The sarcasm was deserved. It carried meaning that I was obstructing an important job we had undertaken trying to help others understand the unobstructed universe, life after life, and the continuing evolution of individual entities. Normally Clair is a true blithe spirit and also a quality teacher. She's been a professor of human anatomy and physiology at a university graduate school of medicine, and a powerful force in bringing us all together . . . you, too, Chris. She's quick to offer help when needed, but also insists that we're involved in a shared assignment - one important to her, essential to us. We're not only convinced that angels dance on the head of a pin, but we're beginning to realize they teach us how they can do it."

For two or three minutes, I sat thinking about dogs and angels on the head of a pin. Then I remembered my anxious need to exchange experiences with these two old men. But the more I thought about our awkward start - Pearl and I - the more reluctant I became. It was Bob again who seemed to sense my problem.

"Chris, did you and your friend try the Ouiji board this week? Tom and I were betting that you'd find a way."

I nodded. "We did. Nothing spectacular - like revelations about dog heaven - but we started off pretty good."

Then I told them about Pearl's shock when our messenger said something only Pearl could know.

"Evidential," Tom said.

"Whatever you call it, Pearl was bowled over. The messenger said YOU DIDN'T TELL CHRIS YOUR FRIEND IS YOUR SISTER."

The two men nodded, as though they already knew about it.

Bob said, "Did you ask who was giving you the message?"

"Yes," I said. "The answer was 'Tony.'"

I saw Bob look at Tom. "Did he say Tony who?"

Then I remembered the third night we had worked the board. "Yes, he did. This time he began the message: THIS IS TONY DEE." And I spelled out the last name.

Tom was smiling. "Small correction, Chris. He meant 'Tony D.' Clair has mentioned him. They belong to the same group."

I was dumbfounded. "The same group? You mean . . . ?"

"That's right," Bob said, "they work in groups.[3] Tony D. belongs to the same group as Clair."

---

[3] see further, *The U.U.*, pp. 58-9.

"Anything else happen, Chris?"

"I got a pencil last night, when I was alone."

"How did that go?"

"I'm not sure. Half the time I thought I was just writing down something already in my head. Maybe somebody was trying to test me,."

"Why do you think that?"

"He or she said, 'WHO ARE YOUR TWO NEW FRIENDS?'

"I said, 'Three new friends.'"

"TWO MEN AND A LADY?"

"I was writing all this down, as fast as I could . . . maybe getting a little bit scared. Know what I mean?"

I was wishing I had gone home instead of using boy scout pacing to get here. Tom's usual smile was encouraging. "I said, 'that's right, two men and a lady.'"

"And then?"

It was Bob who seemed insistent. I looked at him, swallowed twice, and said, "The next message was in a language I can't understand. I honestly don't know what the hell it means!"

There. It was out.

I produced the paper.

Bob read: GALIA EST DIVISI IN TRES PARTES.

He put back his head and started laughing. Tom joined him. I sat like a dunce.

"What's so funny," I asked.

Bob started to answer, but he was seized again with a fit of laughter.

Tom said, "Latin. It's from an early lesson, an introduction to Cicero."

"Cicero . . . what does it mean?"

Bob said. "'Gaul is divided into three parts.'"

Again Tom burst out in laughter.

I began to wonder if they were laughing at me. They sobered up.

"Don't take it personally, Chris. You had a prankster on the wire. He or she is having fun with you. Gaul is divided into three parts . . . and you've got three new friends."

I couldn't believe my ears. Psychic messages that were no more than jokes?

50

Chapter IX

ABOUT NINE O'CLOCK, Tom suggested a break. They went to the coffee machine, I went to the reference desk. Eve was still there.

"How're you doing with your psychic friends?"

"You know them?"

"Sure. They're in here every week." She was looking me over in such a way that I felt like I was on exhibition. "You a wrestler or something like that? Those big shoulders and chest look like it. Maybe you're a model for one of the stores who run ads in the paper."

I don't blush easy. But this girl was not bashful. I was being inspected.. Before I could say anything, she turned to a customer waiting for her attention. After a minute or two of waiting (he wanted a book on 'Kalimantan orchids'), I went to the coffee machine. Bob and Tom had left.

A few minutes later, I was back carrying two paper cups of coffee, and the girl was free. "I didn't know whether you wanted milk and sugar. So I just brought it black."

"What's your name?"

"Chris."

"You missed a chance, Chris. I thought you'd say I didn't need sugar, that I was already sweet enough."

Her laugh was like a soft melody. It didn't explode or sound forced or anything but nice. I'm sure I was blushing now. "You haven't told me your name."

"Eve."

"Eve? Hey, I like that. Pure and simple."

"I'll settle for simple."

I looked at her. Was she trying to tell me something?

"What time do you get off work?"

"Ten, when the library closes."

"Can I buy you a drink at the bar down the street?"

She was smiling. "It sure took you a long time to ask. I'd love to have a drink with you, Chris, and find out what you do for a living - besides read about psychics."

Something about the way she said that made me wonder. "You read about them too?"

"Not me, Chris. I'm Catholic. Not a very good Catholic, I guess. But none of that spirit stuff for me."

I shrugged and turned to leave the counter. "See you at ten. And I promise not to talk about spirits - only the kind you drink."

The melody of her laugh floated up behind me as I left. I stopped and went back to the counter. "Eve, one small request, please. Can you try interlibrary loan for me? I'd like to get a copy of *The Unobstructed Universe*. But it's out of print, and the library copy is being used by Tom."

"Hey, you really dig that stuff. It will take at least three weeks - up to three months."

I decided to say no more about psychic books - unless it came up again over our drink.

When I got back to the seminar room, the other two were already deep in conversation. Bob looked up. "Did you find what you were looking for at the reference desk?"

It was my turn to smile. "Oh, yes! I found what I was looking for."

Tom said, "You took the time needed. Time is receptivity."

I looked at him.

"I lived with the Ashanti for some months," Tom went on. "I was studying their music and dance, especially their talking drum. How it was made and played and how it functioned in society."

I nodded.

"I found out that the quick key to understanding the Ashanti is their rich treasury of proverbs."

"Proverbs?"

"Proverbs. When the parliament gets locked in debate, it's the man with the right proverb who breaks the deadlock. The talking drum recites proverbs, the woven patterns of their kenti cloth stand for proverbs, so do their carved stools and jewelry."

Now suddenly we were in Africa. "You thinking of a proverb, Tom?"

He nodded. "Has to do with time. 'He that has time to morn has time to heal.' Receptivity."

This seemed a long way from my conversation with Eve. I wasn't sure where the conversation might go next. So I just waited. Both men were silent.

Then I said, "Are all their proverbs like that? "Psychology . . .philosophy?"

Tom smiled now. "They cover everything important in life. One of my favorites is a proverb for an Ashanti stool: 'Something that tastes good in the mouth makes you feel good all over.'"

I laughed. "I think I'd like the Ashanti."

Tom was nodding. "You would, Chris, if you took the time to understand them."

Bob spoke up. "Tom made a film about them. It was nominated for a Venice film award."

"No kidding!"

Tom laughed. "Yes, Chris - 20 years after I made it."

I thought about that for a minute. "Are you still telling me something about time?"

Tom nodded. "That's right. Twenty years later or 20 days after the first showing. It doesn't matter. The film hadn't changed. I guess it took that long for word to get around."

Bob spoke up. "That film's in almost every African center in the world - including Africa."

I shook my head. "And it took 20 years to get around the world."

Tom laughed. "Something like that, Chris. But time is really a concept. Sidereal time - the kind clocks keep - and psychological time. The kind that seems to move fast, when you're involved with something interesting."

"Psychological? I don't get it. Time is time, isn't it?"

"Unobstructed time is receptivity."

"You said that before. But what's psychological time?"

I could see Tom was giving it a little thought. "Chris, you were talking to that pretty reference librarian, Eve, during the break. How long would you say?"

I thought about it. "Maybe eight or ten minutes, not counting my trip to the coffee machine."

Tom grinned at me. "Add five for coffee. That would be 15 minutes at the most. Your break was close to a half hour."

"Really?" I guess they had been waiting for me to return. "I had no idea."

"That's psychological time. 'Time flies,' when you're busy talking to someone you enjoy."

"I get it. Like the difference between a long drive by yourself and the same drive, when you're with a friend rapping about something. That it?"

"Right. We can collapse it or stretch it out . . . or settle for receptivity."

I debated whether to tell him I had a date with the reference librarian. I thought maybe I'd come at it indirectly. "Had a nice chat with the reference librarian . . . Eve." I caught Bob's quick look at Tom. "Eve agreed to let me buy her a drink."

"Psychological time," Bob said.

"And I also asked her to help me find a book."

"Oh?"

"I ordered a search on interlibrary loan."

Bob was interested. "What book?"

"The Unobstructed Universe . . . they don't have a second copy," I turned to Tom, "and I'm not going to pry your copy loose."

"Sorry, Chris. I loaned my personal copy to someone a few months ago, and they forgot to bring it back."

"And you forgot who it was?"

He nodded. "When you're ready, I'll bring it back and you can check it out."

I shook my head. "No hurry, Tom. From what you two have been saying, I've got a lot of reading to do before I tackle that. So, I asked the reference librarian to try interlibrary loan. She said it would take any where from three weeks to three months to get it."

"Looking for an answer to a particular question, Chris?"

"Time. I'd like to know more about White's explanation of 'unobstructed time.'" I hoped I'd said that right.

Tom turned his chair toward me. "There's a lot to know. But as a start, maybe something I learned that summer, when I had the chance to talk with Mr. White. I think I was asking about some people who seemed to be able to see into the future."

He sure had my interest now.

"His explanation was simple. He said the curvature of the earth offers an explanation. If it's noon in Boston it's midnight in Hong Kong. If you imagine yourself ascending to the heavens - as high as the astronauts go - then you see the curvature easily. And time is like that. If we think of NOW as straight below us, then look along one line of the curvature, we see the past. The other side's the future. Isn't that simple?"

I thought about it. "You mean that's an 'unobstructed' way to think of time?"

He nodded.

That seemed pretty simple. I'd try it out on Eve. Then I remembered she was Catholic, so we wouldn't be talking about the psychic world. I wondered what kind of drink I should order for her.

"Eve is Catholic," I blurted out.

Bob caught my eye. "How did you find out about that?"

"She told me." I hesitated. "Eve was explaining why she wasn't interested in psychic things."

"Tom," Bob looked at his friend, "tell him about that Jesuit you knew during the War."

Tom looked at Bob, then at me. "I was drafted late in World War II. My training was cut short, and I shipped out as a replacement for the Belgian Bulge. From a replacement depot I went to a blacked-out division. It was spear-heading and about to cross the Rhine. The sergeant said I could find a useful leather pouch, if I looked through the ruble of a bombed-out building.

"I was in the middle of my search, poking through splintered beams, broken plaster, glass, when I noticed another GI sifting through the ruins. He stopped and held out some cards he'd collected from the rubble.

"'Aren't these beautiful?' he said. They were religious cards, a bit too pious for my taste. But I nodded. Later I learned he had been in the Jesuit Order. He introduced himself, and during the fighting war from the Rhine to the Elbe River, we became good friends."

Tom was silent for a moment; lost in thought, I supposed. But when he spoke again, I realized he was trying to find a way to shorten his story.

"I learned a lot from that man. He was a craftsman, hand weaving, leather work, did other kinds of work with his hands. One night we were bivouacked in a building above a wrecked shoe shop. He was making a leather holster for a Czech pistol I'd acquired as a sidearm. Suddenly the building was hit by bombs. The running lath shook, the dim light wavered (we were blacked out at the front window). But he worked on calmly, forming the holster, as though nothing could disturb us. He didn't hesitate in his work, even though glass and splinters were flying all around us. The bombardment lasted about ten minutes. Then it stopped."

Tom was looking off into space, seeing again, I was sure, the havoc of bombing all around him. His eyes focused on me once more. "Chris, we hear rather often about Near Death Experiences. There are many NDEs in a shooting war. And a lot of deaths. But there's no time for introductory travel down a dark tunnel toward a bright light." He looked into my eyes. "Have you heard that line from the bible - 'deliver me from the shock of battle and sudden death?'"[1]

I remembered it, but now it had a different meaning. "You mean . . ."

"Violent death with no possible preparation. The Invisibles have said that frequently a soldier who's been violently killed, goes on fighting. There has been no time for preparation."

Bob said, "Tom, go on telling him about the Jesuit."

"Right. As I was saying, he was absolutely calm during the bombing. In fact, he was like that whenever we were together during the four months in continual engagement with the enemy. I'd never been around anyone with such steady calm no matter what was going on. One night, I said on impulse, 'There's a book I'd like you to read.'

---

[1] cf. *The U.U.*, pp. 43-4.

56

"He waited for me to name it. 'It's called *The Unobstructed Universe.*'" Tom looked at me "'I've read it,' he said. 'One of the most important books I ever read.'

"We talked about it that night and often during the rest of the time spent at the front.. At one point I asked him why the Catholic laity hadn't been told about the concept of an unobstructed universe. He said, 'They're not ready.'"

Wow! From a Jesuit!

Bob spoke up. "I had the same reaction from an old friend of mine who's a Bishop. Same comment: 'They're not ready.'"

Tom said, "That was more than 50 years ago." He looked at Bob. "Bob and I believe the laity's ready now. All the interest in stories about 'angels' saving lives, NDEs, mystical studies. Many people are ready. They're accepting the reality of miracles. A belief in religion is returning. They want to know more. They're looking for explanations."

Thinking about the Catholic laity, I began to wonder whether mention of an unobstructed universe might come up, when Eve and I got to the bar.

Chapter X

WE HAD FOUND a table for two with a dim light. Eve ordered vodka tonic. I asked for vodka rocks. She was talking about her kid sister.

"Joan's only 15," she was saying, "but she knows more about life than I did at 21. I'm 30, Chris."

"I'm 40," I said.

"We've got Joan in a program. She started with marijuana at 12, heroin at 13."

I could see the pain in Eve's eyes.

"But she's gonna be okay. Seven months with the program. Joan'll make it . . . I'm sure Joan'll make it."

Listening, feeling Eve's pain, I had finished my drink too fast. I ordered another, which I was determined to sip slowly.

"Eve," how long have you been at the library?"

"Too long. Six years."

"Before that?"

"Clerking in a Rite Aide for 10 months. Waitress in an Italian eatery for two years before that." She was sipping her drink. "The library's not very exciting - except when somebody wants a rare book for something I never heard of."

"Orchids in Kalimantan?"

"Yeah. I thought it was still Borneo. That guy probably thought I was a lousy reference librarian not to know about Indonesia."

My second drink arrived. I forgot. My first sip was a bit lusty. "Did you go to librarian school?'

"Just one year."

"You got plans - I mean, are you gonna stick with the library?"

She shrugged. "It's interesting, but like I said, not too exciting."

"You looking for excitement?"

"Well, not the way you make it sound." She was looking deep into my eyes now. "It's just that . . . I don't know, Chris . . . I don't even know what the right questions are, much less the answers."

Now what the hell was I supposed to say to that? "Anybody ever fill you in on time?"

I guess she thought that was not a very bright question, from the look on her face. "Time? I'm not sure what you mean?"

"I mean the difference between sidereal time and psychological time?" I thought Tom's information would impress her.

"You mean clock time and fun time?"

I was impressed. "Yeah. I guess you know all about it."

That lovely melodic laugh again. "Not really. I read about it once."

Grabbing at straws I said, "Tom told me that when you and I were talking, during our coffee break, that was psychological time. It seemed like about fifteen minutes. It was more like a half hour."

Those crooked front teeth made her smile special. "Was it really that long?"

"That's what Tom said."

She was studying my face. "Chris, I still haven't found out what you do for a living. No wrestling, no modeling . . . what?"

"Male nurse."

"A *nurse!* Now it's my turn. Are you gonna stick with male nursing?"

"Like you, I haven't found the right questions, yet. I'm taking some course work, maybe eventually a paramedic." I was thinking of the emergency at the hospital. "But, Eve, I'm learning a few things . . . things I hadn't even known enough about to ask questions."

"Like?"

I decided to take a plunge. "Well, once in a while I hear about an NDE."

"A what?"

"Near Death Experience . . . at the hospital."

Eve's face changed. She looked down at her hands. "I've heard about those. They really happen?"

I nodded. "They really happen, Eve. If you hear somebody talk about it, somebody who's been through it, then you're convinced it really happens."

"Ever happen to you?"

"No."

There was a long pause. I guess she was wondering whether I was going to be talking about New Age books.

"How'd you get hooked up with Bob and Tom?"

I told her about the subway, and sitting on a stool in this very bar a couple months later and bumping into Tom. Then the seminar room.

"What do they talk about?"

"In the seminar room?" I wasn't sure how much I should say. "They . . . they exchange experiences."

"What kind of experiences?"

I took another gulp of vodka. "Well, Bob tells us about plants and animals. How some people talk to them. They even talk to one another - trees, I mean."

Her expression told me more than any words she might use. I went on. "Eve, it sounds odd, when I tell about it. But when you hear Bob and Tom talk about it, well, it's not so crazy."

"They're both university men, right?'

"Right."

"Smart?"

"I guess so. Yeah, pretty bright."

"And they're getting you hooked on the psychic world?"

I knew I was squirming in my seat. My second drink was gone. "I don't know whether I'm getting hooked, but I sure want to know more than I know now. Eve, I'm just trying to keep an open mind. The way some of the scientists are doing these days."

I told her Tom's story about the summer with J. B. Rhine's assistant and the professors from Columbia University.

I tried to sound confident. "They tell me university scientists - people with scientific training - are getting serious about these things. They want to know more. Bob quoted White about the problem scientists were having 50 years ago. Something about Galileo and reproducible experiments. I didn't quite understand - except Bob's reference to White's comment that scientists hadn't yet learned to 'work in the nature of the substance.'"

"I don't get it."

"His way of saying their skepticism prevented receptivity."

"Oh. But not the guys from Columbia?"

"Dr. Rhine had invited them to sit in on talks about the thought control of plants. Apparently he knew they would keep an open mind."

She looked at me a long time before answering. "You mean, I *don't* have an open mind."

"I didn't say that, Eve."

"You didn't have to." She went back to her vodka tonic. After two sips, she said, "Okay, Chris . . . you win. What can you tell me about the spirit world?"

The only thing I could think of fast was to order a third vodka rocks. Boy, that was a switch I wasn't set for. I waited for the drink. When it arrived, I took a good big belt of it and began to tell her what I had learned from Tom about the Jesuit and what Bob said about the bishop.

She heard me out in silence. By the end of my telling, both our drinks were nearly finished. Eve reached across the table and patted my hand, like a mother with a six-year old kid.

"Chris, I don't have an open mind. Thinking of my kid sister Joan my mind's full of dead-end questions. I guess I'm a member of the laity who's not ready. Shall we call it an evening?"

I looked at my glass. "Mind if I finish this third vodka? I been putting it down too fast. I wanna sip this one. Okay?"

Her eyes had the look of the mother with the six-year old. "Take your time, Chris." She looked away, then back at me. "Tell me more about your job."

I drank slowly and began telling her about the nice things at the hospital, the patients you meet who need more than the pills and shots prescribed by the doctors. The old man with the stomach pains. By now, I realized Bob had been right, when he said the old man needed me more than the doc.

"You have a girlfriend, Chris?"

This Eve came right to the point. "Not really. One or two I joke with sometimes. But no girlfriend." I was thinking of Pearl. She was a friend. And she was a girl. But not a girlfriend. Not at all what I thought Eve meant.

I got to thinking about that. When I looked up from my drink, there was something in Eve's eyes I hadn't seen before. A reference librarian and a male nurse? It wasn't exactly the kind of pairing old Bob might talk about. She had family problems and I had taken on the pains of a big hospital family.

Maybe we both should have another drink.

"Yes," Eve said. "I will."

I looked at her and blinked.

"You will . . . ?"

"Have another drink. Isn't that what you were thinking?"

Now it was my turn to join the laity. *She read my mind!*

I motioned for the waitress and looked at Eve. "Same?"

"This time on the rocks."

When the drink arrived, I held up my glass in a toast to Eve. "Here's to the first genuine mind reader I ever met!"

I could listen to her laugh all night. We drank to the toast.

I said, "How do you do it, Eve? Read minds?"

The silence was so long I began to think she hadn't heard me. I was about to ask her again, when she answered.

"I was Joan's age, the first time it happened." She was looking directly at me now. "It's happened many times since then. But Chris," she looked anxious, "please understand what I'm saying now. I can only read a mind that's willing to be read." She paused, looked away, then back again. "And sometimes I pick up something that hasn't reached the other person's conscious mind yet."

I guess my look was enough to serve as a question, because she rushed on.

"If the connection's right, Chris, I even know what's going to happen to that person in the future. Not the details. But the large picture. Where they're headed." She was twisting her glass back and forth, but not drinking. "It scares me a little . . . sometimes a lot, and I sure don't know how I catch those glimpses of the future."

Bob's example. Like the curvature of the earth. In a few words I told Eve about Stewart Edward White's explanation.

"Yes! That's exactly how it feels! Like floating high above the time track, so I can look behind at what's happened and ahead at what's going to happen."

This time, when she took my hand, it was nothing like the feeling of a mother and child. I'm no mind reader. And certainly not a psychic. But, for sure, Eve knew something about the two of us sometime in the future.

Chapter XI

THE NEXT DAY, I got up with my head so full of wild ideas, that the only thing I could think of to calm me down was a double header. The Red Socks were looking pretty good for mid-June. I'm not really a baseball fan, but, when I need to get hold of something real, something sharp like the crack of a bat belting that ball high into the stands, those Red Socks will do it every time. So I spent most of Saturday eating hot dogs and drinking beer. In fact, after my day of double headers and beer, by the time I got to bed, I knew I'd go to sleep without any trouble. That was what I needed. The lovely sound of two home runs and a double victory for the home team did it. That was my not-quite-sober reflection, when I turned off the lights and went to sleep.

When I woke up Sunday morning, a vivid dream that pounded me all night was still sharp in my mind. I was on a ball field. Nothing strange about that, after a double header with the Red Socks. Except that I was one of the players. Odd, even for a dream, because I never played baseball, even sandlot. Soccer was my game. A six-foot-two frame and 180 pounds got me on the university team, when I was in pre-med studies.

But in the dream I was on the Red Socks team, outfielder - center field. Here came a hit way back to the fence. I jumped and stretched high and caught it. But, like the crazy doings in dreams, my feet didn't come back to the field. The ball carried me up over the fence, past the bleachers, past the parking lot and out over the city. Way down there were streets and cars and millions of people. All of them looking down. Nobody was looking up. I waved and yelled and kept going on up higher. Nobody noticed. Nobody looked up.

I hung on to the baseball for dear life. I knew if I ever let go, I'd fall all the way back to those little cars and figures hurrying somewhere, without once looking up.

It wasn't dark yet, but the light was strange, up there in the sky. I kept studying all the busyness down there. All the action below looked like windup toys. Heavy traffic, freeways, five tiny little squad cars chasing somebody. I kept floating up and up and things were getting so tiny they looked like ants. Then I couldn't see them any more, just a smear, a blur of what I knew was still busyness. Gradually I began to see the curvature of the earth. Just like Bob's explanation. I was still hanging on to that baseball like grim death. Somehow, it kept me from falling out of the sky.

Then loud and clear someone said, "Chris, take a good look. The next time you see this, it will be different. And so will you. As a start, look for the right reference. Try the Park at night. 'Night' can be spelled with an 'e.' Take a good look, Chris, and remember what you see. The way time curves behind you and before you, like the earth. Remember what you see, Chris. Remember all this."

With a gentle release of the baseball, I woke up in bed, in a cold sweat, trembling. Why? Was I frightened? Not exactly. But I was hanging on to the bed sheets like a life rope. I laid there a long time, got sleepy, and dozed off. Then it began again. Same dream. The hit to center field, catching the ball, flying off into the sky, five squad cars chasing a black panel truck - I was watching everything happening below, until I could see again the curvature of the earth. That voice kept talking: "Remember this. This is important. Night can be spelled with an 'e.' When I woke up, I was sweating and trembling.

All day Sunday, I moped around the apartment, went out for a walk, couldn't stand the noise and traffic. Cars and people, lots of people, all looking down, just like in the dream. Sunday afternoon, late spring weather, everybody was out. Walking, driving, jogging. Sirens! More sirens! Then came a squad car racing down the street chasing a shiny convertible.

66

I stood watching them roar down the freeway until they were out of sight. I still stood there, noticing that everyone I could see was looking down. At nothing, really, just looking down in front of them, while their minds were busy with something else, somewhere else. Just like the dream.

Then I remembered "Night can be spelled with an 'e.'" How could that be? "Nightie?" I must be losing my grip!

Sunday night, I thought about getting drunk But that didn't feel right. I thought I might call Pearl to tell her about the dream. But that didn't feel right either. Eve was the next thought. But that was one I didn't know how to handle. She said she could read minds - minds that were willing to be read. Sometimes she knew things that would happen in the future. Just the broad picture, whatever she meant by that. She understood my story about Bob explaining time and the curvature of the earth. Yes, she said, like looking down on the time track.

There was a basketball semifinal game Sunday night. I drank a little beer again, and the excitement of personal fouls and time-outs and a near fist fight made me forget about the curvature of the earth.

Until Monday night about a half hour before I got off work. A call came to the hospital for me - from Eve. Would I buy her another drink, when the library closed at ten? She wanted to hear about the ball game.

"You knew about the double header on Saturday?"

"A friend of yours, Pearl, said you weren't working Saturday. Off to a double header."

At least there was nothing mysterious about her knowing there was a ball game on Saturday..

She spoke again. "On second thought, Chris, it can wait until Friday night."

"What can wait?"

The phone went dead before there was a reply.

Chapter XII

THE REST OF THE week at the hospital was a rush. There were many emergency patients after a tornado struck the edge of the city. At the end of every day, I had a quick bite to eat after work and was in bed by nine o'clock. No time or energy left for baseball dreams or basketball finals. But by Friday at six o'clock, I was ready to go to the Park I had clam chowder and took some crackers for the pigeons.

A few minutes after seven, I saw Tom coming up the path in the Park. Bob wasn't with him. We nodded as we met and continued down the path at a slow pace.

"Bob coming?"

"Not tonight. He's a grandfather. Tonight's a birthday party."

"Grandfather! I hadn't thought about Bob with children and grandchildren. When he talks, the things he talks about . . . I never think about age."

Tom was smiling at me. "He's a *great* grandfather. Speaking of age, a close friend of mine, who lived to be 92, never got old, mentally. He was younger in attitude than most people your age."

"Your talking about the information age, computers, the internet?"

"He took that in stride easily. But I was thinking of the human condition - a truly rare understanding of other human beings. He had an instinct for knowing things about people that they didn't know themselves."

"Can you give me an example?"

"Yes, one that you might say is very 'modern,' even for today. He had a young daughter seventeen, who told him at breakfast that she was in love with a man and was going to marry him. She said he was separated from his wife - his third wife. And as soon as the divorce was final, they would be married.

"My friend suggested that his daughter and the man live together. His daughter said the man was between jobs; his wife spent all their money. They couldn't afford to rent a place. My friend offered to let them move in with him. It was large house. Five bedrooms. He promised he wouldn't be in their way.

"The man moved in. My friend was careful to finish breakfast and be out for a walk when they got up in the morning. If they were around the house in the day time, he found an excuse to be gone. He fixed his meals either before or after the two of them ate. The situation was as close to being alone as if they had rented the house."

"Did they get married, when the man's divorce was final?"

"After three months, the man moved out and was not heard of again. The daughter went on a trip to Mexico with a girlfriend. And Chris, like Bob, my friend was a great grandfather, too."

I was thinking I didn't know any other fathers who'd do something like that.

Tom was steering us toward the library. "Without Bob, there's not much point in sticking around the Park."

We entered the library, and I nodded to Eve, as we passed the reference desk on our way to the seminar room. We sat down, and I said. "Look, Tom, if you'd rather wait until next Friday, so Bob can join us - and Clair, too . . ."

"Nothing on your mind, Chris?"

Was he guessing? I'd been waiting all week to tell him and Bob and Clair about my dream. "Just a dream I had."

"Do you want to tell me about it?"

For the next five minutes, I described in detail everything that happened in my dream. He was very attentive. I told him about waking up in a cold sweat, dozing off, and the same dream happening again. He seemed interested when I mentioned several times that everybody was looking down.

When I told him about the voice and what was said, exactly what was said, Tom asked. "Was it a man or woman?"

I sat there feeling stupid. I didn't know. When I told him that, he nodded.

"Any idea what it means, Chris?"

"None. Tom, I've thought about that dream all week long. What does it mean?" I looked at him. "It *does* mean something, doesn't it?"

"I think so . . ." He seemed to be in a deep study. "It may take a while before you understand it - all of it. Dreams are complicated to understand. And those still with us the next morning are usually significant. People tend to brush them aside, unaware that a dream, a memorable dream might be an attempt at communication."

"From the other side?"

"Yes. Especially when you hear the repeated phrase 'this is important, remember this.'" He lowered his voice, as a man entered the seminar room and sat at one of the tables. Quietly he asked, "Have you tried to spell 'night' with an 'e?'"

I blinked. "Not really. Do you think it means 'nightie?'"

He shook his head. "'Evening' is spelled with an 'e.'"

Evening . . . evening, eve. Wow! Eve! Of course, Eve!!! But what did that mean? "Do you think that means 'Eve,' the librarian? The voice said 'reference,' too. Tom, am I on the right track?"

"You plan to tell Eve about the dream?"

I nodded. "Especially if she's in it."

After a pause, Tom said, "It reminds me of a dream I had, when I was 19. Twenty years later I understood most of its meaning. But it was another 20 years before I understood it well." He shook his head. "About now, it's been still another 20. I'm beginning to get the full implications."

"Sixty years to understand a dream! It must have been important."

"That phrase, 'remember this,' was also in my dream. Chris, you'll think of it again over the next few years. Depending on your receptivity, one day you'll understand it. The conditions you noticed - for example, everybody looking down - mean something. I'm sure there's a lot more to it than we could guess. Maybe the name 'Eve' was something for you to figure out.

I shot him a quick look. Did he know more than I did about Eve? This was a subject I'd rather not talk about . . . not now. "What was *your* dream, Tom, when you were 19, and what happened after 20 years and then another 20? And now?"

He was smiling, as though it amused him to go back to an experience when he was 19.

"Like you, I had a powerful dream. It was a demanding dream. Although the night it happened, I didn't understand much of the demand." The way he looked off into space, I could imagine he was seeing that dream again, after all these years.

"I was traveling above a narrow highway," he said, "not floating, not consciously flying, just moving forward above the road but following it, as though I were being guided by it. The countryside around me was not familiar. It was barren, desert-like, some mountain ranges in the distance. The sky was bright and clear, morning light, I think, and you could see for miles. It was a vista I'd never seen before. Not at all like the green Rocky Mountains I had loved the year before in Colorado."

He looked back at me, as though to anchor his telling to an audience. "For sometime I traveled above the road, guided by it and steadily climbing. I reached a kind of summit and turned and looked back. Then I heard a voice. I, too, didn't know whether it was a man or a woman. As I stared back at the road I'd been traveling above, the voice said, 'Everything on this side of the mountain is one thing. Remember this. It is important.' Then I turned and looked ahead. The voice said, 'Everything on the other side of the mountain is something else. Remember this. It is very important.'

"I looked at the road down below me, over which I was traveling again. It turned to the right at the top of the crest, and as it descended in a winding direction, I took particular note of the several peaks that lay ahead. I was aware in the descent that the road turned left, so I was again headed in the same direction I had started. All the time I kept hearing the voice: 'This important. Remember this. Everything on this side is one thing, everything on that side is something else. Remember this. It is important.'

"The next morning, I woke up with that dream strong in my mind and the phrase 'remember this, this is important' still sounding as it had been pronounced by that voice. I'd had psychic experiences since childhood - I told you the one at age six."

Tom returned to his dream. "I got dressed and went down to breakfast. The voice heard in the dream was still in my ears: 'this is important.' So I told my mother about the dream. She listened sympathetically. I didn't know what she thought about it. She usually listened to my fancies and dreams sympathetically. So, we had breakfast, and nothing more was said about it.

"Three weeks later, the brother of an uncle-by-marriage stopped by my house. I was home from a freshman year at the University of Colorado, and all fall had been doing some writing. It was early January. I had to be reminded by the man that he was a distant relative, since I probably had not seen him more than once or twice before. He said he and his wife and a male friend were driving to California. He'd heard from my uncle that I was home from the University. Would I like to go for the ride? One week going, one week staying in Los Angeles, one week returning. I was in a writing slump, and I had been curious to know more about California. So I asked, 'When are you going?' 'Tomorrow morning at six,' was his answer. I checked with my mother; my clothes had just been washed. I said I'd be ready."

I was trying to anticipate his story. "Were you still thinking of the dream?"

"No, Chris. I'd forgot about it. The excitement of driving to California was a lot. Remember, this was a long time ago - before freeways and four-lane highways. I remember that the road over the Continental Divide in Colorado, in those days, was a narrow two-lane road.

"The next morning we started out over the snowy roads of the mid-west, and the second day came to drier landscape in the flat lands of the West. The third day we had left the wintry snow blankets of the mid-west far behind and were entering desert country in Arizona. My uncle's brother's wife and I were riding in the back seat. Suddenly I was on the highway of my dream. I looked around at the landscape and recognized it in every detail. I think the little hairs had risen on the back of my neck.

"I turned to the woman beside me and said, 'I'll bet you a dollar I can tell you which way the road turns over the crest.' She looked at me. A dollar that long ago was a lot of money for a young man 19 years old and unemployed. When she hesitated, I added, 'It turns to the right, winds down the grade, and there are four major peaks ahead of us.'

"She nodded at the bet. As we continued up the incline, I turned to her again, hearing that voice of my dream, and said, 'I'll bet you another dollar I don't return with you, when you go back home.'"

I was sitting up straight by now, waiting for the punch line.

"I won both dollars," Tom said. "Why I stayed on in California is another story. I didn't return to the mid-west until 27 years later for a five-day visit."

"What did the man and his wife say, when you told them you weren't returning with them?"

"They were surprised, but when I explained I'd be enrolling at the University, USC, they said no more about it. I never saw them again. I don't even recall their names."

"Strange this man dropped by unannounced and offered you a ride to California. And you really didn't know him."

"He'd heard that my father died when I was young, that I was home with nothing to do - in those days in the mid-west writing was not taken seriously. Of course he didn't know he was driving me to a new life, one totally different from being born and reared in the mid-west. Maybe that voice I heard in my dream also got through to him."

My mind was back on my dream again. What did my dream mean?

"Ready for a coffee break?" Tom asked.

"I want to know about those two 20-year happenings that helped you understand your dream. And this new 20-year mark - what has happened that makes you think you finally understand all of the dream?"

"Okay, after the break. I imagine you want to tell Eve about your dream - especially since she may have been in it."

Chapter XIII

WHEN I GOT TO the reference counter, four other people were waiting to see the reference librarian. Eve nodded at me with a quick smile and went back to her customer. I decided to get my coffee and left.

At the machine I saw Tom again. He was already sipping his coffee.

"Is Eve busy? Friday night's usually a big night for the reference librarian. Some University students in summer school want to get their homework done tonight, so they'll have the weekend free."

I nodded and lined up to wait for the coffee machine. I could feel Tom's eyes on me, even though I wasn't looking at him. I finally got my coffee and walked up to him.

"Can you make a start on that first 20-year mark? I'd really like to know what happened that would shed some light on a dream two decades earlier."

Tom looked at the busy traffic around the soft drink machine and the coffee machine. "We might as well go back to the seminar room. It's a little easier to talk in there."

When we entered the room, we saw that one of the tables was occupied with a meeting of five university students, who seemed to be planning some kind of rally.

"It's a nice night for a walk, Tom. Okay?"

Outside the air was balmy, the stars bright, the hum of traffic the only distraction, one you learn to live with and can turn off. "The end of the first 20 years," I said.

"I have to start a little earlier, so you'll understand why it was a breakthrough." He hesitated, as though trying to decide where to start and what to omit. "Prior to entering the army I was a mixed up man in his early twenties: writing, acting, white-washing fences, selling Hoover vacuum cleaners, and playing in a society dance band. For five years I worked in the aircraft industry along with the music, writing, and acting. Then the army." He glanced at me. "That was preceded by an amazing evening spent with a psychic medium. Sometime we'll talk about that. Abruptly, my infantry training for the South Pacific was cut short. I shipped out as a replacement for casualties of the Belgian Bulge. Very quickly I was involved in a shooting war with horrors and destruction and constant death all around me - I was one of the soldiers to open Buckenwald. I landed in a hospital in Paris shortly after VE day in Europe.

"I was in no pain. 'Battle fatigue,' they called it in World War II. In the first World War the name was 'shell shock.' All I was supposed to do was lie in the sun, read, and go for walks. Early in that two months I realized it was the first time I could recall that I was not allowed to *do* anything. Just relax. Just learn to get through the wild nightmares that jarred me several nights a week. For the first time in my adult life I had time to think. Time is receptivity, remember?"

I thought about that. Tom's way of looking at time was different from the use most people make of it. Receptivity. I wasn't sure what he meant.

"To shorten the telling of a couple of month's deliberation let me simply say I reviewed my life - remember the 'life review' people talk about in an NDE? Well, my life review went on for most of that two months in the hospital. I began to understand that I'd been so busy at so many things I hadn't got hold of anything. So, I began to eliminate. If I had to let go of everything except one thing, what would it be?

"It took a lot of sorting and sifting. But it always came back to music. If I could settle for only one thing in life, it had to be music."

We were more than a block away from the library. Tom said, "Shall we be heading back?"

"Was that your understanding of the dream? That music was what you should be doing?"

"No, Chris, that was only a beginning. Even while dodging bullets and bombs at the front I found some time for automatic writing. But messages that came through, typical of such communication, were deliberately vague. For example, before the time in the hospital, one message said 'learn the kind of song you'll sing, when you return.' I'd been involved with music back in the mid-west, and had done some singing, along with playing sax, clarinet, and flute. Yet, in the middle of a shooting war, I knew the message didn't relate to a career in jazz.

"After spending two months in the hospital at St. Cloud near Paris - thinking, re-evaluating, walking, reading, pondering - one thing was clear: I knew for sure that music was an essential part of what I had to do that would make 'everything on this side of the mountain one thing and everything on the other side something else.' Music was the foundation of understanding my dream."

"So you went back to music."

"Well, not in the same way. Before the army it was jazz. That stretch in the hospital made me want to know more. So when I returned to civilian life, I began to study musical composition with a famous composer. That lasted five years."

"So that was the difference. You became a composer."

Tom was smiling. "No, that still wasn't it. Oh, I wrote quite a bit of serious music, some of it published. But occasionally during the five years I would say to my famous composition teacher, 'I have the feeling it isn't enough . . . being a composer. I ought to be doing more.'[1]

"I guess that was a brazen thing to say to an internationally famous composer. But we had become close friends. And I was trying to be honest with him and myself. Then there was an abrupt change. He announced he'd be going to Europe for an extended stay; I decided to go back to the university and finish my education. After an M.A. in composition, I spent two years in Europe and took a Ph.D. there."

---

[1] cf. *The U.U.*, p. 55, and see further Chapters XV, XVIII.

Tom stopped as we were about to enter the library again. "Chris, maybe that's enough for tonight. You can probably get Eve's attention now."

"Wait a minute. Was that it? A Ph.D. in music?"

Tom shook his head. "Not quite. I didn't know until a couple of years later what was fundamentally different on this side of the mountain. I found out in Java. A few days after I landed there."

I guess he saw my frown.

"We'll talk about that another time, Chris. Just to end the story for tonight let me say that was the beginning of my identification with music of the world, not just the masterworks of my own culture. All the musics of the world made this side of the mountain totally different from the other side."

"Can you give me a hint what happened 20 years after that?"

Tom looked strangely serious. "If you remember, I said that there were many instances in World War II of soldiers experiencing a Near Death Experience, with no time for the dark tunnel leading to a white light. A stroke at age 60 was my NDE - but there was no need for the tunnel and light. Other forces were involved."

I guess I was still frowning.

He laughed. "Maybe some other Friday, Chris. Meanwhile give some thought to your dream. And talk with Eve about it. She might have a clue."

At the reference counter I waited until Eve finished with a customer. I looked at my watch. "Another half hour, then we have a date at the bar, right?"

"Maybe just a walk. There's almost a full moon tonight."

Our walk took us back to the Park. "If Bob were with us," I said to Eve, "he would explain how all the living things in this Park are able to communicate with one another. Listening to him, I sometimes think these plants get the message across clearer than we two-legged animals can manage."

We found a bench. We sat close, thighs touching. The moon was bright enough to see her smile. "Chris, besides the double header, what happened to you since we last met?"

"I had a dream . . . sorta puzzling. I'm not sure what it means."

"Oh? Tell me."

I told her every detail about the dream. She had no reaction. "Eve, do you have any idea what it means?"

"No. Do you?"

"Only that I'm sure it's important for me to remember. Tom was telling me about a dream he had when he was 19. Said it took 40 years - maybe 60 - before he understood it completely."

I looked into her eyes, trying to read whatever she was thinking. "Eve, Tom helped me figure out that 'night' spelled with an 'e' is evening or eve - or Eve." I was hoping for a reaction. There wasn't any.

"Your name - and the word 'reference' - you?"

"What makes you think my name was implied?"

There was suddenly a lump in my throat. I was short of breath. "Why did you want to go for a walk in the moonlight, instead of sitting in a bar?"

I knew that wasn't a very good answer, but it got close to what I was feeling.

Chapter XIV

THE NEXT WEEK was filled with daydreaming. I went through all the right motions at the hospital, no mistakes - but my mind was elsewhere. The dream kept coming back. I was puzzled why Eve's name was in it. That moonlight night in the park we did some serious talking. Nothing binding, really. But we were candid.

I also thought about Tom's dream and his struggles to understand it for 20 years. No, for 40 years. If we got around to talking about it again, maybe for 60 years! If I had to wait that long to understand my dream, I'd be 100!

Thursday afternoon Pearl stopped me in the hall, as I was on my way to the lab with some urine samples.

"You got time for a break pretty soon? In the rose garden?"

I was surprised. Pearl and I hadn't had a chance to talk much since our last go at the Ouiji board a couple of weeks earlier. "Sure, Pearl." I glanced at my watch. "In 15 minutes? About 4:30?"

It was 4:40 before I got to the rose garden. Pearl was sniffing the tight buds of a bush near the end of the garden. When I reached her, I noticed that many had opened, since our last visit. They were a reddish orange.

"Smell good?"

"Naw, these hybrids. No smell."

We found a bench, and I waited for her to take the lead. Funny how you keep seeing the same people every day, nod to them, pass a wise crack . . . but never know what's going on inside their head. I was wondering about Pearl. She came right to the point.

"That book you were reading a month ago, *The Betty Book*, I checked it out of the library. I've read most of it. It's interesting"

I was surprised. "It's a good one to start with, Pearl. Are you convinced they were on the level? No faking?"

She gave a long sigh. "Yes . . . and the thing I like the most . . . they warn you. If Sis had read that book, maybe she wouldn't have got herself in trouble. They talk about trouble makers. Remember that guy who thought the communications he was getting on the races were money makers? He kept using the messages to place bets. And every time a winner. Until they set him up and he lost his shirt."

"I remember.. I'm trying automatic writing now. But I work hard not to expect anything, not to ask specific questions, like 'should I quit my job and try a different trade?' or "will I make out with the girl I'm seeing at the library?'"

That slipped out before I thought.

"Is she the one I talked with last week? Eve?"

Then I remembered her mentioning the call the day I was at the ball game. I nodded, keeping my eyes on the roses. I wondered where Pearl was heading.

"Chris, would you be free for supper at my house tonight? I've been trying automatic writing, too. I'd like to show it to you, see what you think."

"That's great, Pearl! Sure, I'll come for supper. I don't know much about all this yet, but the two people - three people - looking over my shoulder impress me more every time we meet."

Pearl was on her feet again. "Okay, Chris, that's what I wanted. My house about 7:30?"

Pearl was a good cook. She didn't offer me a drink before supper. She said we'd better keep a clear head for the rest of the evening. I missed beer to go with the spare ribs and sauerkraut and corn bread. I passed on the apple pie, but she had a piece. Watching her eat and thinking of how much sugar she piled in her coffee I had trouble imagining her doing automatic writing.

I offered to dry the dishes. It was a quarter to nine before we sat down to look at her automatic writing.

There were five messages. I felt I was not the one to evaluate them, the way Bob or Tom could. But as a starter, I asked her whether she had some other samples of her handwriting. Apparently she had anticipated the request, because she handed me another sheet of writing. When I compared this with the messages, it didn't take a handwriting expert to see they were different.

"That's very interesting," I said, looking at the way the 'o's, 'e's, and 'a's were formed. The difference was striking. The 't's and 'l's were also different. "Pearl, it sure doesn't look like your handwriting."

I was reading the words. Some of them didn't make much sense, until one message began explaining that the writing was the work of a group, several people on the other side working together. I looked up at Pearl at this point. "Working in groups. I've heard Bob and Tom talk about that at the library." I finished reading them, pulled one from the collection. "Did you ask questions?"

"I tried not to - except to ask who was doing the communicating."

"And that's when you received the explanation about a group. What about this one?" I held up the sheet I had separated from the others. It said, "We need more time . . . difficult to explain . . . later."

She gazed at the writing. "I guess that was when I asked if someone would tell me what had gone wrong when my sister got screwed up."

Pearl was looking at me almost as though she was pleading. "She's okay now. But I wouldn't want her to get involved again."

"I'm too much a beginner myself, Pearl, to give you advice. The best thing for you to do, if you're still trying to understand how your sister got in trouble, is to do a lot of reading. The old ones, all the so-called *Betty Books,* the new ones, published as part of the New Age publications. That's the safe way to start."

I could see she still wasn't very happy with my response. "Stewart Edward White wrote a little book, which he said was made up of answers to questions in the many letters he received from readers. I just returned it to the library. It's called *Anchors to Windward.* Try it. It might have the answers you're looking for."

The roses surrounding us were strong and vibrant - yellow, peach, red, white, persimmon, lavender. I thought Bob could explain to me how they communicated. Pearl wasn't noticing the rose blossoms. I decided not to mention what I'd been hearing from Bob - at least not until I understood it better myself.

"How was the double header?"

"Won 'em both! Best day at the ball park this year."

"You a play baseball, Chris?"

"No, not my game."

I was thinking of my dream and wondered whether I should tell Pearl about it. I remembered Eve's comment about wrestling. If I told Pearl I played soccer, it might sound un-American. "I dream about baseball, sometimes."

You dream about it? About playing baseball?"

"Not exactly playing ball . . . just hanging on to one."

"Funny dream, Chris."

"I guess so. But it might be important."

I knew by her look I wasn't connecting. I decided not to mention the dream. "Try *Anchors to Windward*, Pearl."

Chapter XV

THE NEXT NIGHT was Friday. I got to the Park late, just as Bob and Tom were leaving for the library. As I fell in step beside them, Bob said, "I hear you had a dream, Chris."

"And from what Tom tells me, I may have to wait 40 or 60 years to figure out what it means."

Tom laughed. "Hold on, Chris, I was talking about *my* dream. You may begin to understand yours any time. After all, you're about twice as old as I was, when I had my 'this-is-important, remember-this" dream."

"I'm glad to hear you say that. Using your calculations I could be 100 years old before I know what it means."

"Did you talk with Eve?"

"I did. She was no help. Said she didn't know why her name might have been implied in the dream."

For a time, the three of us walked along in silence. Then Tom spoke again. "Maybe Eve thinks *you* should figure out why her name might have been intended in the dream. After all, Chris, it was *your* dream, no one's else."

I was remembering Eve's statement that sometimes she could see into the future. Not the details, she had said, just the general happening. Was she holding something back?

"Think of it this way," Tom was saying, "Just stick to one part of the dream. Eve's name. Why might her name have been intended in the dream? Think of that part of the dream as a riddle.

In Java I learned that a favorite form of solo song is something called *majapat*. These are songs sung for children - not children's songs, but songs sung for children, a form of education. The words are usually a riddle. It's up to the child to figure out the meaning. It's a beautiful form of education."

I thought about this. Okay, so I was a child. In this business I certainly was a child. "In other words, you're saying it's something I'm supposed to figure out."

"If somebody else told you the answer to the riddle, they'd be depriving you of the opportunity of learning something. Chris, it's *your* riddle."

My dream, *my* riddle. Part of a dream for educating children. This was one of the times when my new friends were getting over my head. In fact, as I thought about it, that was most of the time. Maybe I should hand something back to Tom. "Tom, that's the second time you left me stuck in Java. Assuming you've solved all the riddles in *your* dream, don't you think you should fill me in on this 20-year revelation in Java?"

We walked along for some time in silence. I began to think maybe Tom had been offended and was not going to say anything.

"Chris, have you ever heard of a movie called "Living Dangerously," "The Year of Living Dangerously?"

I stretched to remember. "Yeah, I think so. It was about a bad time in Indonesia. Revolution, kicking the Dutch out, dictatorship . . . right?"

"I was there during that year, in fact, for two years. When I arrived, the British Box Club was still in existence,. There were proper times to wear white coat and tuxedo pants. It was the last edge of colonialism. And the deprivation, the illnesses, annual famine in Java - the average life expectancy of a Javanese male was 33. I attended a number of Muslim funerals for young men I had got to know.. There was malaria, polluted water, starvation. Not a very good time for an idealistic would-be composer to land in Java. I arrived with 15 pads of empty score paper for full orchestra. Two years later I left Java with 15 pads of score paper - as untouched as the day I arrived.

"One night in the British Box Club, white-tie dinner dance, I sat at a table for ten. Two or three of us were just watching those who were dancing. One was a cultural attache' from the American embassy. I had been in Java only a few days. But the want, the need was so great, I was depressed looking on at the opulent crowd in the British Box Club. I turned to the attache' and said, 'I'm only a musician. There's so much poverty . . . I wish I were here in some capacity to help.'

"He had been in Indonesia almost two years. I'll never forget his answer. 'Young man, you're the lucky one. You'll get to know these people through their music and dance.'"

"And he was right?"

"Chris, the simple answer is 'yes.' But the two years that followed were so filled getting to know the Javanese - as well as a very different society, the Balinese - it would take hours to answer fully. It was the first time I had lived in an epic society. It required a different orientation to almost everything."

"Epic? You mean like in long stories?"

"Yes, a society that finds its identity in the behavior and beliefs of the gods and heroes of great literature told and retold as shadow plays and dance dramas, solo songs and dramatic excerpts. Both these societies believe this literature is the story of their own ancestry. Individuals take pride in claiming kinship with epic characters. The late President Soekarno identified with one such figure known as *Gatakatja*. The identification is so firm that comparison of someone to 'Bima' or 'Arjuna' or 'Gatakatja' or 'Rawana' immediately provides typical traits of character and association with heroic or demonic deeds well known to everyone.

"This great literature is founded on a complex of religious overlays: animism, cult of the ancestors, the culture hero Panji and his relatives, Hindu stories of the Ramayana and the Mahabharata, and in Java a thin topping of Islam, in Bali a strong layer of Balinese-Hinduism. There is also a very small minority that is recently Christian."

"You said an epic society requires a different orientation to almost everything. Can you explain.?"

"A quick answer would be that these societies, like all societies, have an unique set of values and sanctions. But the differences are sometimes so subtle that we Westerners are unaware of them. The daily evidence of this is everywhere, readily present. Someone from the West - a non-epic society like the United States - could unknowingly offend by trivial behavior and action, possibly a dozen times in a half hour."

"I don't understand."

Tom frowned. "As I said, a thorough explanation would take a long time. But a couple of simple examples in social behavior: in my first long residence in Indonesia, a male who stood with folded arms across his chest or hands in his pockets or laughed loudly or, when introduced, pronounced his name clearly - these common actions of the American male would have been judged insulting behavior by the Javanese."

"Today? *Still?*"

"A gradual awareness of foreign manners has softened the abrasive effect for the Javanese; but down deep they still regard them as marks of coarse behavior."

"You learned all that through music and dance?"

"Yes, through literature, dance dramas, even the Javanese language, which in its most formal sense has nine levels, some of them so different they are mutually unintelligible. The Javanese identify with a code of behavior associated with the *priyayi* class of nobility during the period of East Indian colonization. This highly regulated behavior was adopted by the Javanese nobility and copied by millions of commoners as the model of refinement."

I felt like I was back in a university lecture hall. But I was curious about the difference between what he called epic and non-epic societies. "Tom, you and Bob talk about time, about our obstructed sense of time and the unobstructed essence of time, which you say is receptivity. Is that different in Java and Bali? You said they had a different orientation to almost everything."

"Very important point, Chris. When I landed in Java I had been introduced to the psychic world of the White books, to the great man himself, been through a war, where the things I'd been hearing about were greatly intensified by the shock of continual combat. Naturally I was wondering what I'd find among the Javanese and Balinese."

He hesitated, looked over at Bob, back at me. "Your question was about time. It's quite complicated. An anthropologist has described epic societies as polychronic societies, non-epic peoples as monochronic. I'll give you an example. If you've set your mind to be somewhere at a certain time, like the first time you tried to be at the park at seven, it bothers you mightily, when something interrupts - even something as important as the old man with stomach pains. We non-epic people are clock watchers, terribly aware of the hands of the clock. In epic societies, polychronic people, they are able to step out of one time sequence and enter another without a twinge of conscience. Let's say you are about to leave for a dinner date, when somebody drops in unexpectedly. A Javanese gives no sign that he's gong to be late for an appointment, even though formal dress might hint that's he's gong out. He chats with his unexpected visitor, serves him tea and tidbits, and passes the time of day until his guest decides to depart. It would be rude, if he were to indicate that he's late for a date elsewhere. And the Javanese host expecting you would understand that something had come up to detain you. The priyayi ideal would demand that you be the perfect host, suppressing any anxiety about the time, until your guest decided to leave.."

"And that's being polychronic?" I know a guy from Thailand. Every now and then he's very late and never bothers to explain. Epic society.

"If the polychronic person views time differently, does that affect his understanding of the essence of time as receptivity?"

I wasn't really sure how to say this, but I was sure Tom would get my meaning.

He nodded. "I think so . . . if he understands the unobstructed view of time." Tom smiled at a recollection, I assumed. "Yes, I got to know several Javanese who understood that receptivity is the essence of time - but their understanding was tempered by their polychronic orientation."

I shook my head. "I don't get it, Tom."

He laughed. "Don't worry about it, Chris. The concept is difficult enough for us clock watchers, never mind the fortunate ones who can manage a "poly" orientation to time."

"You say fortunate?"

He smiled.

As we walked on toward the library I thought about Tom's words. He was a musician, a world musician. He understood things about other cultures that most people are not aware of. He was still talking.

"Contact with another culture through music and dance is the most direct way to learn a people's true identity. Like understanding the subtle implications in the idioms of their spoken language, which are learned growing up in the culture. Yes, the cultural attache' was right. I certainly bypassed the protocol that ruled his life at the embassy."

I stopped walking. "Tom, I think I'm beginning to understand your dream. Your mission on this side of the mountain was getting to know people, all kinds of people, through knowing their music. Was that the meaning of your dream?"

"That was the beginning. I worked on that assumption for the next 20 years, then came my guarded - not guided - NDE. We'll talk about that some other time."

I looked over at Bob. "You know about all this?"

"And more. I know what happened 20 years after that."

The rest of the way to the library we didn't talk. I kept thinking about the riddle in my dream. If frustration made me a child, I wasn't very grown up that night.

Chapter XVI

WE TOOK OUR USUAL SEATS in the seminar room, and Bob spoke up. "Chris, if Tom spent 20 years trying to understand his dream, trying to find out where he was going, be patient. Don't push. Just relax, and you'll be shown the way."

His gentle voice helped. "I'll work on it. How was the birthday party?"

"Special My granddaughter's eleven. After blowing out the candles and unwrapping the presents, she looked at me and said, 'Grandpa, what does that word "poltergeist mean?"' She's in the seventh grade. Somebody had asked the teacher, and the teacher couldn't explain it."

"What did you tell her, Bob?"

"I said a poltergeist is literally a noisy ghost that sometimes plays tricks on people. She wanted to know if some ghosts are quiet. I assured her that most of them are. The noisy ones are like the malcontents you meet at a soccer match."

Remembering news of some European soccer matches I could relate to that. It seemed to fit what I had heard about poltergeist. "Is it true they're attracted to children?"

"I've heard that, but I think it's a little twisted. Children are very open, receptive. It's quite common to hear their stories of psychic experiences. Most adults put it down to childish imagination. Unfortunately growing old too often hardens both the arteries and the imagination."

Tom laughed out loud. "No one can ever accuse you of that. Bob, for a change of pace, tell us about your correspondence with J. B. Rhine. I think Chris should know about the beginnings of the Department of Parapsychology at Duke University and acceptance by the scientific community of ESP. He might want to read some of the publications."

Bob said, "Okay, I'll mention that briefly. But Chris is more likely to be interested in Dr. Rhine's interests that *weren't* published. And the professor of philosophy from a major university, who came to Duke to 'expose' him as a fake."

I was all ears to hear more, when suddenly I saw a change come over the professor. He was not looking at either of us, but staring straight ahead. "Sorry, " he said, "I just got a sharp tingle from Clair. She's got something on her mind."

After a pause, he went on. His voice was the same, but the style of his words had changed. I jumped, when I heard my name.

"Chris, do you remember what I said to you through Bob, when attempting to explain the difference between your time, space, and motion and the same time, space, and motion employed in my unobstructed half of our one and only universe? I said, in effect, that we, by means of higher frequency, are capable of 'manipulating' time, space, and motion through their respective essences. Remember, the essence of time is receptivity, the essence of space is conductivity, the essence of motion is frequency. Put in those terms, we're capable of 'molding' them to where they are no longer obstructions to us - though they continue to be to you. Thus, by 'collapsing' your time, space, and motion to our advantage, we are only a thought away, should you call for our attention.

"No great mystery here. Through your own evolvement you have already penetrated to some degree the obstructions of time, space, and motion by inventing radio and satellite relay stations that are either stationary or orbiting in outer space. Thus, you can communicate around the world almost instantaneously, and these are only the beginning of newer miracles to come. Through continuing evolvement you are daily thinning the 'barrier' that separates the obstructed half from the unobstructed half of our one and only universe.

"Now, Chris, you still wonder how some people can communicate directly with one of us while others cannot. How do you really know they cannot? How do you know *you* cannot? It's said that one person out of five is born psychic, and that any one of the four remaining can develop a psychic capability if they so wish. In other words, all of mankind is psychic to one degree or another.

"Your psychic potential is higher than you realize.[1] Go back to when you explained to Tom and Bob why you couldn't meet them at the park on time due to a problem at your hospital. You said an old man in pain held on to your wrist, wouldn't let go. You felt it was important that you stay until the doctor arrived. Remember what Bob said? 'The old man needed you more than the Doc.' Now, that kind of attitude may not qualify you as a recognized psychic, but it's a large step toward becoming one through further development. That alone will have you conversing with 'angels' in due time. A little practice makes it possible."

I gulped and was silent. Tom was silent. Then Bob went on, now in his own usual style of talking. "I spoke to Clair about angels. She tolerates my reference to her being one - accepting it as more of a compliment than a 'title.' She made it clear that she has yet to meet one in the theological sense, inferring that there are many high enough evolved to more than qualify for such a title. She is a bit hesitant to talk too much about things she has still to learn, emphasizing that her immediate task is to work with us in getting the continuity of life message across, stressing the need to further evolve toward narrowing the 'gap' between our two halves of the one and only universe. Progress toward that aim is becoming more evident. The more that the obstructed half learns about the truth of immortality, the higher will become their collective consciousness, and once that goal is reached, the laws of the unobstructed universe will be universally understood and abided by."

Bob hesitated. "I'm doing a lot of talking - Clair and I. But there's one more important point she made. It was in response to my concern that we, the obstructed, usually fail to acknowledge the continuity of those who have passed on.[2] Betty White made reference to that failure to understand that the newly unobstructed are very much alive with feelings equal to our own. Clair put it nicely. She said, 'We pray to God for both help and thanksgiving.

---

[1] cf. *The U.U.*, p. 60, in which Betty explains that everybody is more or less psychic.
[2] see further, *The U.U.*, p. 201.

We do it because it soothes the soul. Yet we rarely pray to our "dearly departed" to assure them that we know of their new eternal life and their well being. Rather, we weep over their loss, causing them sorrow for our lack of understanding. They would much rather receive full understanding of their new position in life, even encouragement to move ever onward. Open communication through prayer, even direct thought, becomes reciprocal, for "we departed" want most to encourage those left behind to become assured of life's continuation and to fill their existing life to the fullest with conscientious intent.'"

I looked at Tom and he at me. We both nodded at the same time and said, "Time for a break!"

Then suddenly, half out of his chair, Bob sank back with a grunt. "Okay, okay! Sorry about that!" He looked at us both. "I sure got the message strong that time. Clair hadn't finished."

His voice had a firmness about it now. "We are attempting to communicate in areas not easily understood by those not familiar with the unobstructed universe. Terminology alone is strange to them. We must find easy-to-understand words that explain deeper meanings we ourselves struggle to grasp fully. I must depend on a higher authority to best translate these concepts into anecdotes suitable for the average reader. Not all are versed in the science of physics.

"The accepted use of the word 'essence,' the being or essence of a thing, from the Latin word 'esse' or 'to be' - that which makes something what it is - was adopted by the team of authors of *The Unobstructed Universe*, and not without considerable discussion. Now, we must stand on that decision and help our readers realize that they exist in the obstructed half of our one and only universe, and, therefore, they are obstructed by the great trilogy of time, space, and motion. TIME, they never have enough of it to get things done. SPACE, they have to transcend it to arrive at their destination - and that takes time. MOTION, getting a move on to get to where they are going in order to be there on time. Obstructions, obstructions, obstructions, a trilogy of them!

"We, in the unobstructed half of our one and only universe, negate your obstructions of time, space, and motion by operating within their essences. The essence of time being receptivity, the essence of space being conductivity, and the essence of motion being frequency. The word 'frequency' is best understood when considering its wide use in your field of physical science. In our unobstructed phase we, too, use frequency, but to a much higher degree. Higher than your science has yet to conceive, yet, through the evolutionary process, that frequency will in time be better understood, as you already understand how radio waves pass through solid walls.

"Taken in order: Receptivity, received in time, is the ability or capacity of the mind for receiving impressions. With that gift we receive your thoughts in our mind as quickly as you direct them to our attention - and only then. In other words, we receive them only when you ask that they be received by us. Your mind is your own, as is your free will. However, be mindful that your free will is governed by your conscience, your innermost thought, your consciousness, your moral sense of responsibility, for only *you* are responsible for knowing the difference between right and wrong in accordance with accepted man-made or universal law."

Bob stopped. He looked at me for several seconds, then said, "Chris, all this is really intended for you But I confess, both Tom and I are also learning - even though we think we know these concepts well. Are you too fatigued for Clair to go on? Shall we ask her to postpone the rest of this talk about time, space, and motion until next week?"

I shook my head quickly. I was thinking of Eve's explanation of how she could read your mind. . . . only a mind willing to be read. Sometimes something that hasn't reached the other person's conscious mind yet . . . what's going to happen in the future. Was all that involved with Clair's explanation of receptivity?

"It's deep stuff, Bob. But the sooner I get the message the sooner I can be thinking about it, trying to understand. Please ask Clair to continue."

The invitation was not necessary.

"We, by employing the essence of time, 'collapse' it to our needs. We reduce it to where it does not exist as you know it. No magic there, you do much the same when you reduce time psychologically without realizing it. For example: You find the person sitting next to you on a nonstop flight from New York to San Francisco to be an excellent conversationalist. You exchange experiences and become so involved that you are both amazed to learn you are suddenly on final approach to your destination. Where did the time go? It psychologically contracted. You not only used it to great advantage by making a new friend through exchange of interesting adventures, you also psychologically collapsed not only sidereal time, but also sidereal space to where it too seemed inconsequential; and as far as motion was concerned, it too became psychologically enhanced.

"Consider the extent of evolution that made the physical aspects of the cross-country flight possible - without psychological advantages. Consider also the almost miraculous pace of present day evolution, and then imagine what new advancements will appear in the near future. And then stop and realize that all of this was predicted in that informative before-its-time book entitled *The Unobstructed Universe*, written back in 1940. The content of that book, in spite of its deep but still comprehensive message, was first of its kind to reveal life as lived by we who dwell in the unobstructed half of our one and only universe. And if the reality of this seems inconceivable in the minds of your most highly educated, then ask them if they do not dream of a frequency that would make the theory of a fourth dimension possible? Remember, it was Albert Einstein who postulated that it is that very dimension that could well be man's dream of heaven. Today's laboratories, caught up in the swell of evolution, are unknowingly working toward that very end, for one discovery leads to another. That's what evolution is all about."

Tom held up his hand suddenly. "Hold it, Clair."

I jumped at the intrusion, thinking Tom was surprisingly bold or rude - if not both. Then I saw that he had a tiny micro-cassette recorder and needed to reverse the reel. He looked at me, after changing it. "Sorry, Chris. But Bob and I want to have a record of this exactly as Clair states it." Anticipating my question he added. "Sure. We've taped all previous messages from her."

The moment the recording was turning again, Clair continued. "Conductivity, the essence of space, is what makes it possible for 50,000 plus angels to dance on the head of that previously mentioned pin, and if that speck of space can be called the 'Conductivity Ballroom,' think of a name for space left over to accommodate the uncountable ever-growing population of our entire unobstructed universe. Think of space in our world as limitless, having no boundaries, only points of reference, which we transcend through thought alone. Again, no great mystery. You do it all the time when day-dreaming of an unforgettable vacation in another land - the vision, the color, the sound, even the smell. For a few moments of your time you were actually there, and in being there you all but eliminated time, space, and motion in making it possible - even though it was accomplished psychologically.

"The next time you allow yourself the luxury of a vicarious visit somewhere faraway, pause and remember that it is made possible through your ability to psychologically collapse time, space, and motion in getting there; and then be aware that you too have experienced the reality of the essences of time, space, and motion through the omnipotence of thought alone."

Chapter XVII

THE FOLLOWING FRIDAY I asked to get off early, so I could take Eve out to supper at five. She had to be back at the library by six, so we settled for a fish-and-chips place, crowded, noisy, but great food. The noise and the crowd kept our talk at the level of chit-chat, until we were back outside, walking toward the library.

Eve was holding my hand as we walked. I liked the feeling. I didn't know where we two were headed in the future, but somehow I was relaxed with the idea that there would be a future for the two of us. She stopped suddenly and let go of my hand..

"Chris, you didn't mention your dream once during supper."

"We keep so busy at the hospital and I'm so frazzled by the time I get home, I don't think about it. I haven't thought about it more than once or twice this week." I took her hand again, and we went on walking. "I guess I'm getting like Tom. Maybe in another 20 years I'll figure it out."

"Have you thought about the riddle?"

"No . . . I can't get to first base." I caught myself, remembering it was a *baseball* dream. "I mean I have no idea what it means - except 'e' for Eve sounds right. You had any thoughts about that?"

She only shrugged her shoulders, and we walked on, each of us thinking, I guess, about that damn dream. Funny how you get stuck on a simple thing like that, and it keeps on going around in your head, once it starts.

We reached the library. "Chris, are you coming in to wait for your friends?"

My watch said 6:05. "Think I'll head for the Park. That'll give me about a half hour to listen to the trees talking before Bob arrives and translates."

I watched her disappear into the library and found myself thinking again about the dream. Everybody looking down. I turned around and headed for the Park.

I found a bench in the Park near the dogwood tree Bob talked to. Since listening to him about how live and responsive nature is, I was seeing things differently. Or maybe I should say, I was beginning to see things for the first time. The bark on a tree had become a live thing for me.

Bob's dogwood was younger that another one 15 or 20 feet beyond it. The bark for the first seven or eight feet was marked by small vertical and horizontal indentures, as though someone had carefully prepared an elaborate checkerboard for tit-tat-toe. Then above that eight-foot mark the bark was suddenly smooth. The leaves were veined and fairly broad, a fresh green that seemed to radiate health. The other dogwood, older, but not much taller, had tit-tat-toe markings much farther up, with only the top few feet showing a smooth surface. The leaves were smaller, partially closed, several of the branches were dead.

Looking from one tree to the other I decided the older one looked tired. Probably had some kind of infestation. Bob would know. He hadn't been talking to that one. Did it feel neglected? Did trees have feelings? I began to imagine what it must feel like to be cut down with an ax, sawed off with a chain saw. Then I thought about the extensive logging I was reading about in western states. The occasional commercials on TV that showed tiny little plantings in the name of reforestation. As though those pitiful beginnings were some kind of apology for cutting down huge 100-year old veterans of the forest to line the pockets of the lumber industry.

I shuddered and decided to concentrate on some of the day lilies planted in concentric circles of reds and yellows in several beds in the Park. I looked at my watch. Bob and Tom should be along any minute.

As though he'd read my mind, and as I said before, I was beginning to know he could, Bob came up behind me.

"Chris, have you been talking to my dogwood?"

There was something in his voice that made me wonder. Had he somehow tuned into my thought about the pitiful attempts being made in the name of reforestation? I didn't have long to wait to for an answer.

"Have you ever wondered," he said, "about the projects in reforestation? You know the difference between 'clear cut' and 'select cut?' Let me tell you."

I recognized the tone as an introduction to professorial wisdom. Tom came up behind him, winked at me, and went off to a nearby bench.

"Clear cut," Bob said, "is the kind of cutting that distresses the public. Every tree is cut, so all that's left is a vast spread of essentially bare land. 'Select cut' is the term used, when only certain trees are chosen for felling."

His pause, I decided, was made for me to respond. So I said, "Well, at least some of the logging shows a little sense in 'select cut'."

Bob nodded toward the bench Tom had found. "Let's sit over there by Tom. I want you to understand why 'clear cut' is not as bad as it sounds. If you consider the scenic gains, it opens up vistas to mountain ranges, dramatic landscapes, miles of nature's splendor not visible when the forest obstructed your view."

I was a little disappointed. Did old professor Bob really think cutting down a forest was justified by opening up the surrounding scenery? But he hadn't finished.

"Of course that's a small bonus compared to the intelligent planting and tree selection that is essential in reforestation. Usually only two types are chosen: Ponderosa and Douglas Fir. They're carefully spaced, so there's proper room for rapid growth."

I thought about it for a moment. "Okay, Bob. I see your point. Proper spacing and only two types of pines means reasonably fast growth."

"Conifers," Bob corrected. "One's a pine, the other a fir."

I nodded, amused at his habit of precise language.

"It probably assures a much better environment than was there before the cutting. There are no tan oaks, for example, which in the wild often crowd out other noble trees and dominate the landscape."

"Tan oak?"

"Used in tanning, Chris, the bark, which yields tannic acid. But the tree's not good for much else." He smiled at some afterthought he was having. "Unless we remember that the Indians used the acorns for making bread. And some landscape planners like to include the tan oak near homes to ensure a large shady tree for the property. Much shade, exactly what makes them undesirable in a forest of conifers. They blot out the sun needed for healthy growth."

I had a crazy question. "Bob, you think those new little trees planted in reforestation have things in common with your dogwood? I mean, you think they appreciate and respond to the care given to them in guaranteeing another forest in the making?"

Bob laughed and turned to Tom. "Tom, Chris is catching on fast. Yes, Chris, they respond to the same flow of energy, the same unobstructed forces of time, space, and motion that control my little dogwood."

Tom wasn't smiling. "And Bob, we should add that Chris and you and I are continually responding - usually without know it - to that same flow of energy."

Chapter XVIII

IT WAS ALREADY 8:30, by the time we reached the library. On the way to the seminar room, I waved at Eve as we passed the Reference Desk Her smile would keep me lighthearted until our ten-o'clock date. Meanwhile, based on words and phrases dropped as we walked from the Park, I suspected Tom and Bob had some heavy talk in mind for the next hour or so.

The seminar room was empty, except for a middle-aged woman copying recipes from a cook book. Her streaked gray hair was tied in a bun at the nape of her neck. She wore no makeup. She didn't even glance at us, when we found our lounge chairs at the other end of the room. At the sound of Bob's opening remarks, with precise and firm moves she folded her book, picked up her notes, and left the room without even a glance. I had a hunch she was a good cook.

"Chris," Bob said, "Tom and I think we should summarize some principles germane to our discussions." He held up a book. "It's all right here in *The Unobstructed Universe*. It may take a while for you to get around to reading it, so we thought we should try to give you some basic points."

Bob cleared his throat. "First, a few simple facts. You and Tom and Eve and Pearl and I were born with a fixed quality of consciousness. Fixed, Chris, and each one quite different.. During the obstructed phase of our individual evolution we can't change it one whit. We're who we are for as long as we live in this obstructed part of the universe."

I took a deep breath. "See if I understand. Something like the idea of DNA? You're who you are, no matter how hard you try to change, for as long as you live. That it?"

Tom spoke up. "Part of it. The old sources White depended on[1] explained that consciousness is the only reality. You can think of it as the 'I-am' reality."

He stopped and unfolded what looked like a page from a magazine. "A couple of years ago there was a great interest in a competition between a computer they named 'Deep Blue' and the world's top chess champion, Garry Kasparov. People weren't sure they wanted the computer to win. Some thought it would. *Horizon Magazine* published a lengthy article featuring a discussion among five men. Knowing we'd be talking about consciousness tonight I brought an excerpt. Lanier and Hitt are talking.

"Lanier points out that the special quality of a human being is having an awareness of being conscious and a belief that a person might be able to contact other consciousnesses.

"Hitt asks what he means by conscious.

"Lanier admits that it's hard to talk about, saying that consciousness is 'the experience of experience itself.' He makes the point that if a computer could simulate the interior of the brain and the way neurons behave, even then consciousness itself would be lacking."[2]

"Wait a minute. You mean if we could make a computer function like a brain, program it in such a way that it could look at the behavior of the brain's neurons and duplicate all that complicated activity, what we mean by consciousness still wouldn't be there. Is that it?"

Tom nodded, looked at Bob for assurance, and went on. "Bob referred to the *quality* of consciousness. But that's only one half of consciousness. The other half of the concept can be called the *'quantity'* of consciousness. The 'how-much' of consciousness. And that half is something we can do a lot about - develop it, increase its how-muchness. You're given a fixed quality, which

---

[1] see further *The U.U.*, pp. 75-81.
[2] "Our Machines, Ourselves, " discussants: Jack Hitt, James Bailey, David Gelernter, Jaron Lanier, Charles Siebert, *Horizon Magazine*, May, 1997, pp. 53-54.

you can't change during your life time; but the *quantity* of consciousness - the 'how much' - can be developed according to your talents, to the limits of your quality of consciousness. The example given was Tony the ditch digger and Einstein.[3] Both were born with a fixed quality of consciousness. For each of them the challenge was to develop their *quantity* of consciousness, to the best of their ditch-digging muscles or capacity for science, given them at birth."

I thought a minute about Tony and Einstein. "Are you saying that if Einstein had goofed off and Tony had worked like hell to be the best ditch-digger around, are you saying the scientist didn't increase his quantity much, but Tony did?"

When Tom nodded, I added, "I don't mean any disrespect, but I have to say 'So what!' One is still Tony and the other is Einstein. Right?"

Bob jumped in fast. "Yes, but because Tony has increased his quantity to the maximum, he can expect to raise his *quality* of consciousness in the unobstructed universe. If an Einstein did not utilize his talents living in the obstructed half of the universe, he would have accumulated very little moral strength to develop his quality of consciousness in the unobstructed universe."

Tom added, "And, Chris, that's what it's all about. The individual in evolution. We're born with given talents to do a particular job.[4] The more fully we're able to fulfill that obligation - and it *is* an obligation - the more easily we can evolve further in the unobstructed universe."

Well, I wasn't sure how much of that I understood. But one thing didn't sound right. This idea of developing quantity - I was thinking of all the guys and women, too, who didn't seem to have even a foggy notion about developing anything. Just have a good time. Live it up, drink it up, shack up with anybody - jeez, what a messed up world was going on around me.

I excused myself and went out to get a cup of coffee. I really needed something stronger. The more I thought about what Bob and Tom were saying the more bothered I became.

Back with the coffee I sat down without acknowledging their presence. But I could feel them looking at me.

---

[3] see further *The U.U.*, pp. 79-81.
[4] see further *The U.U.*, p. 55.

Bob said, "Too much, Chris?"

"No, not really. I think I understand your pitch, but . . ." I was stumbling badly, "well, I've tried to be honest with both of you and these ideas . . . well, if I hadn't already heard some of the other things you've talked about . . ."

Tom said, "Okay, Chris . . . finish your thought. If you hadn't heard some of the other things?"

I decided to spit it out. "Sorry, guys, it sounds like Pollyanna to me. If you dig your ditches as deep as possible, everything's sweetness and light. You make it sound like a do-gooders' world."

Shit! I was downright depressed. And I'd been thinking all along that these two were regular guys - even if they did talk like college professors. I tried to remember what Eve's beautiful smile looked like.

I stood up and looked from one to the other. "Let me say it again . . . I really am sorry you guys, sorry as hell. For a few weeks, I had the notion maybe I was headed in the right direction." Men don't cry. But damn it I was fighting tears!

Tom stood up and began turning pages fast in the book *The Unobstructed Universe.* Bob was still sitting, mouth ajar, as though he wanted to say something but couldn't get it out.

Tom said, "Give us another minute, Chris."

I stopped, half way to the door.

"You've made more progress than you realize. Listen to a few words that put it better than either Bob or I can manage."

He began reading:

"Each individual is put into the world to do a job, and he comes here best and happiest only when it is completed; "

Tom interrupted himself. "'Here' refers to the other side, the unobstructed side."

" after he has gathered to himself as nearly as possible his requisite of work and experience. The purpose of the present divulgence is to restore in earth consciousness the necessity of individual effort, and the assurance that the effort will not be wasted. The only assurance of this is a return to the belief in immortality. "

He paused to let it sink in, I guess, then continued.

"A second purpose is to instill into earth consciousness the oneness of the whole. THIS BROADENS YOUR ETHICS AND

RESTRICTS YOUR MORALS. Both have been too loose for the comfortable living of mankind. Incidentally, one of the causes for the instability you note in peoples, individuals, society, thought, art, is the ultra and sudden ease of communication in time and in space. The use of radio, the automobile and the airplane is not stabilized. They have been too rapidly developed and perfected for the assimilation of society in general. Knowing these things even better than you, it could not, therefore, be our purpose to do more at this time than reestablish on the basis of your present knowledge - and the needs of your present knowledge - the faith in the validity of self that is tottering."

I looked from Bob to Tom and then back again. I waited for one of them to speak.

Bob broke the silence. "Chris, that was written in 1940, 60 years ago. Think of the advances made in communication skills and outer space since then, and remember how fast they have been developed. Nothing has stabilized. I suppose never in the history of man have morals and ethics been looser than now. Morality? If developments were too loose 60 years ago what are they now?"

I thought about the cries of alarm and protests of free speech when the internet began to include unfounded news reports, extremes of yellow journalism, pornography, the Starr Report. What was it the book said? Instability in peoples, individuals, society, thought, art . . . .

It suddenly had become like watching a cliff-hanger video, then the lights go out. I asked, "Is there more?"

Tom nodded. "Lots more, Chris. But let's finish this thought. After mentioning the need for helping to promulgate ideas for the scientist, the communication continues:

"It is only through the application of the reality of law, the acceptance of responsibility by the higher quality, the recognition of the need of the lower qualities or aid in their individual fulfillment of their work and obligations, that the world can settle into a true evolutionary process. It is important not only for you, but for us, that this occur."[5]

Tom and I were still standing. Bob's mouth was closed now, and he was looking at both of us.

---

[5] *The U.U.*, pp. 55-6.

I sat down in my lounge chair and was suddenly aware of a worn spot in the old oak floor. These vast thoughts were whirling through my head at hurricane speed. If I got it right, as one of their jobs the Einstein qualities had a responsibility for the Tony qualities to help them work on the how-much idea. I sure was no Einstein. But I wasn't exactly a Tony either. Wherever I was between the two of them, if there really was something to this idea of evolution, I began to realize that part of my job - and I hadn't figured that out yet - but whatever it turned out to be, I had a responsibility to find ways to help the Tony qualities develop their "how-much."

I looked from Bob to Tom, and stood up slowly. "Thanks, you two . . . and whoever said what you read to me. Sorry if I seemed to blow up. But thanks for reading that stuff."

Once again I started toward the door. Then I turned back. "I've got a walking date with Eve at ten. I'll see if I can explain to her what I've been hearing. Sometimes things come clear, when you try to explain them to somebody else."

Chapter XIX

THURSDAY AFTERNOON AT THE HOSPITAL was like a nightmare. Most of the time I was on the first floor helping with emergency cases, so many that the sound of those swinging doors began to make me cringe. Worst pile-up of cars in 20 years, the papers said. It sure was the worst day I'd ever spent in that hospital. They asked me to stay on four more hours. I dragged out of the entrance a little after ten and walked home.

Instead of over-time pay I had settled for the next day off. So, Friday morning, after a huge breakfast of my own pancakes and sausage, I donned shorts and a T shirt around eleven and headed for the subway. It wasn't too crowded at that hour. I had only one transfer to reach the JFK Memorial Library. I wasn't planning to read or even go inside. But I liked the openness, the view of the water, the distance from heavy traffic. I needed to think.

From the subway station I took the bus to the U Mass Boston campus (University of Massachusetts, Boston) and enjoyed the hike over to the Memorial. I stayed outside, located a stretch of green grass with a good view. Out over the water, way up high, there were masses of clouds bunched together. They were white on the edges, a little darker toward the middle. A high-elevation wind was moving them pretty fast. I sat there, hugging my knees, staring up at the clouds and their Rohrshock patterns until my neck got stiff, maybe twenty minutes or so. I lowered my gaze and began rubbing the back of my neck. I heard somebody come up behind me.

"Chris! I thought you'd be at work! What're you doing over here? JFK research?"

It was a guy I'd known in school, when I spent some undergraduate time at U Mass Boston. I motioned to a spot on the grass next to me. "Hi, John. Join me?"

He sat down. John was tall and skinny.

"No research - I think my research ended when I had to leave my second graduate year in med school.. And you? Did you finish at Hopkins?"

Somebody said he went on to graduate work in Baltimore at Johns Hopkins. Probably an M.D. by now.

"Last year. I'm doing an internship up here. I heard you were working at the same hospital."

"I'm a male nurse. One more course and I'll qualify as a paramedic. You like what you're doing?"

"I thought Med school was rough, until I started my internship. Frankly, Chris, I'm not sure you're supposed to like being a doctor."

"Internist, right?"

"Good memory."

I didn't know how to keep this conversation going. "Once past the internship, when you start seeing the same patients on a regular basis, you'll like it, John." I looked at him, remembering the Tony and Einstein story. Both of us were somewhere in the middle. "When your patients turn into people," I heard myself saying, "you'll begin to know why you went through all the shit to become a doc."

He laughed. "Haven't changed bit, Chris. Tell it like it is, right?"

John got to his feet. "Sorry I gotta run. Maybe I'll bump into you sometime at the hospital. I've known you were there ever since my internship started. Funny we come way out here to meet for the first time since U Mass Boston."

I watched him go, then fixed my eyes on a sail boat not far off shore. Friday. Whoever was sailing that boat didn't have to work for a living. It was too far away to tell whether the two people at the tiller were young or middle-aged or old. And what the hell were they doing to increase the how-muchness of their

110

consciousness? Were they put on earth to sail a 37' sloop? Was that their job? Who assigned these jobs? Your DNA?

The big mass of clouds out over the water was turning black. The light summer breeze had changed, beginning to blow a little hard. The sloop had lowered the main sail and was still moving briskly with nothing but the jib catching the wind. One person was tying down the sail. Was that his or her job in life?

I thought about John and Einstein. And me and Tony. Jealous? I guess, a little. If Dad hadn't died when he did, maybe I'd be right there along with John, doing my internship. Like him, asking whether a doc was supposed to like being a doc. Shit! Well, another course and then a paramedic. Doing something on the spot that might make the difference between life and death. Not exactly an MD . . . but getting closer.

Then for no reason I began to think about my baseball dream. Remember this. This important. I was flying out over the city again, tall buildings getting smaller, toy cars moving bumper-to-bumper in liquid streams, little people all looking down. John had been looking down, when he sat with me for a few minutes. Looking down during the pre-med years, during med school, and still looking down as an intern. He hadn't noticed the Rorhshock clouds. And what if he had? Were they telling people something? Something connected with how-muchness? Not with everybody looking down.

I guess the couple on the sloop felt the threat of heavy atmosphere, the picked-up wind, higher waves. But they, too, probably didn't take the time to study the Rohrshock puzzles in the threatening clouds. They were looking down. At the tiller, the beam of the main mast, the deck, the increasing wave activity. Looking down.

Why was everybody looking down?

Feeling heavy inside I got up and started back for the University bus stop. Where the students and the professors and the yard workers and the kitchen help were all looking down, headed for their next class or a late lunch or a bed of flowers - jobs they were put on earth to do?

How do you get answers to questions like that? Like Tom, wait 20 years or 40 or 60?

By the time I caught the bus and then the subway and got home it was late afternoon. I walked into my two rooms, went straight to the phone, and called the Reference Desk. When Eve answered, I said, "I'm looking for a recipe book for a spicy dish made with green mangoes, red peppers, vinegar, and a little sugar. I hear it's from Indonesia.. Can you help me?"

The melody of her wonderful, warm laugh blew away all the storm clouds, pulled everybody's head up to listen, brought me back in touch with reality

"Chris! How come you're not working?"

"I took the day off, and I can take you out to dinner. Five o'clock okay?"

The song in her laughter was still in my ears after I hung up.

We settled for hamburgers, fries, and a Coke, so we could eat, walk, and talk at the same time. Half way through the burger I realized we were walking toward the Park. We had settled for a walking supper so we could talk. Funny, but Eve had said little, and I couldn't seem to get started.

By the time we got to the Park and found a bench, the food was finished. I looked into those warm black eyes and said, "All the things I told you about last Friday, the ideas Tom read in *The Unobstructed Universe*, I guess I sounded pretty mixed up."

A quality about Eve was becoming familiar to me. Most of the time, if you left some things unsaid, she seemed to get them anyhow. Right now I had the feeling she was ahead of my tangled ideas. I had a strong hunch she understood more than I did about working on your how-muchness, so when you knocked at the pearly gates you were ready to upgrade who you were, that slow climb from Tony to Einstein. "Did I get through to you at all?"

She'd formed the habit of holding my hand, when we were sitting on a bench. I liked that. There was something reassuring about feeling the warmth of her hand in mine, even when we weren't saying anything. I remembered the old man with the stomach pains. Eve had helped me learn that the power of touch was very strong medicine.

"Was I communicating?" I asked again.

With a quick little move she kissed me on the cheek. "You were communicating," she said, "maybe more than you knew. The hours I spend answering questions at the Reference Desk - some of them dumb - finding books I never heard of, telling about things I never heard of, watching the satisfied smile, when the customer has the book in hand . . . all of that, Chris, is part of the growth of your quantity of consciousness. You're helping someone, their need often adds a little nugget of knowledge to your quantity . . . it's a two-way process. You give and in giving grow with the return that's always part of the giving."

She squeezed my hand. "Am *I* communicating? Is that what Tom was talking about?"

A two-way street. You give and receive in the giving. And that helps the how-muchness grow. "Thanks, Eve. You make it sound simple. Whether you dig ditches or your garden patch or work on the theory of relativity doesn't matter much. It's doing what you're good at doing and helping others in *their* doing at the same time." I kissed her on the cheek. "In fact, the more I think about it the better it sounds. Everybody likes to do what they're good at doing - reference librarian, male nurse - and chalk up credits at the same time."

She slipped her arm behind my back and gave me a hug. She had been carrying a flat mailing envelope with her ever since we set out to eat. I was curious, of course, but decided she'd mention it, when she was ready. Her soft musical laugh accompanied her outstretched hand with the mailer. "Here, Chris. This is for you - maybe for us. Didn't take as long as I thought it would. The timing's good."

I slid an interlibrary copy of *The Unobstructed Universe* out of the mailer. Eagerly I began to flip through the pages.

"Chris," Eve said, "I sneaked a preview look at the book, when I wasn't busy at the Reference Desk today. Read page 78. Its a communication from Stephen, who was the contact from the other side in an earlier book,[1] directed to Stewart Edward White."

I found the page and began to read aloud.

"Postulating earth-life as quantitative evolution, Stephen proclaimed the other 'half of evolution' to be qualitative. Thus he established for Consciousness - the one and only reality - two planes or, better perhaps, two modes; QUALITATIVE EVOLUTION, or life there as he knows it after what we call death. His plane, or mode, of consciousness, he said, is qualitatively free; quite as our earth plane, or mode, of consciousness is

---

[1] *Our Unseen Guest,* Harper & Brothers, February, 1920

113

quantitatively free or, at most, subject only to such limitations as result from the fixed quality of individuals and species.

"On the basis of evolution, then, and evolution's own need to account for its mutations, the Stephen philosophy asserts a qualitative plane or mode of existence as an inevitable necessity of the development of these mutations."[2]

---

[2] *The U.U.*, p. 78.

Chapter XX

AFTER I WALKED EVE back to the library I decided to skip a return to the Park and go instead to the seminar room to wait for Bob and Tom. I got there about 6:30, and it was deserted. I sat at one of the tables and opened *The Unobstructed Universe*. The first few chapters were easy to read. They were mostly talking about "evidential," a subject I didn't feel much need to worry about. Chapter VI, WE SET OUT,[1] continued that lead, but began to get down to cases.

Stewart Edward White's wife Betty, now in the unobstructed universe, announced that she would be working through Joan, who had been the psychic medium who delivered the Stephen philosophy.[2] Betty had worked with her before she died, which she said had been a preparation for her present assignment. At one point, she put forth the startling idea: ". . . death is much simpler than birth, it is merely a continuation. Earth is the *borning place* for the purpose of individualization. That is one of the things I am to tell you about later."[3]

Before I finished reading the chapter, Bob and Tom walked into the seminar room.

"We missed you at the Park," Bob said.

---

[1] *The U.U.*, p. 39.
[2] see further *Our Unseen Guest*.
[3] *The U.U.*, p. 44.

"Eve and I were there earlier. She got my book, so I decided to come here and start catching up on my reading. I'm about half way through Chapter VI.."

Tom's smile was in place. "Wonderful, Chris. You've almost reached the beginning."

Bob had found his easy chair, and Tom and I pulled up beside him. He seemed to be a little preoccupied.

"Chris," he said, "I've got a recent note from Clair, which she asked me to read to both of you. Something you may know about at the hospital. NDE's."

I shook my head. "Pearl, the Registered Nurse, knows more than I do. I know mostly what I've heard, not what I've seen."

Bob seemed anxious to come to the point. "This is what Clair gave me on the computer last night:

"You ask about my views of NDE's. A valid question, but answered with qualification. Obviously, *I* never had a Near Death Experience, for the reason there was nothing salvageable of my body to return to. Riddled with the ravages of cancer I was wasted beyond repair. You saw that at your last visit, and I read in your mind your wish that I be released from my suffering. I understood. Do you remember my last words, whispered because I wanted you to understand? Realizing how awful I appeared to you, and knowing that you struggled bravely to make me feel that it didn't matter, I said the only thing that came to mind to alleviate the truth that I was at death's door, fully aware that my skeletal appearance told you so, for a woman's vanity cannot be masked. Yet my words did wonders for your deep depression. You suddenly brightened up on hearing me say: 'I am trying to remember all that was written in *The Unobstructed Universe*,' followed by 'I love you.' That was when you left, knowing there was no need to return, for you knew then that I knew that soon we would speak to each other again."

For several minutes Bob was silent, starring vacantly at the computer-generated pages in his hands. I glanced at Tom for a clue. He shook his head, so I knew there was still more to come. A moment later, Bob continued reading.

"Each day in your half of our one and only universe you continue to evolve. By now you are becoming aware that NDE's are not new. They have been occurring since the beginning of mankind. Only now are people admitting to such experiences. Science, still unable to explain an NDE, is unavoidably cognizant of ever-increasing reports of their occurrences, and that presents an enigma, for [because] science, due to reputation, evolves at a mind-boggling pace. Miracles, unexplained, continue to happen, as do NDE's. Is it not reasonable to admit that truth of NDE's has previously been suppressed due to nonconformity? Why now is it almost fashionable to admit to having had one and, better yet, understand more of its intended purpose. Each day you evolve!

"NDE's are not all alike.[4] They vary according to the individual. Even identical twins have different fingerprints. Objective of the NDE remains the same, but the mode of action differs, a characteristic of mankind's molding. As with the few negative experiences suffered by users of the Ouiji board, so are there less than enjoyable memories reported by some who have had an NDE, though they are rare. Again, testimony of differences in man's makeup. Set patterns in the minds of some are difficult to erase. Seeds of doubt germinate as do the great majority with positive potential. The recent book you have been reading [Death's Door], telling of the variables of NDEs, is but a beginning of other books to follow. Further evidence of continued evolvement.

"It is our wish that you do not have to suffer the pain of near death so often associated with an NDE. Nor do we wish to encourage anyone to experiment with an NDE with the intent to preview life beyond. That becomes automatic when your rightful time arrives. Near Death is only what the name implies. Being sent back from the brink of death is intended, and as more statistical evidence of NDE's is complied, you will discover that attitudinal change of survivors is predominantly for the better, and though some will complain about their return, missing the peace and tranquillity the experience offered, they will learn that fulfillment of life's assignment is a far better reward."

I noticed that Tom had been watching Bob closely and was not surprised, when he interrupted. "Bob, your throat must be getting dry. Let me bring you a drink of water. Or would you rather have coffee?"

---

[4] A variety of types is presented in Jean Ritchie's book, *Death's Door*, mentioned earlier.

"Except for the color and temperature they're the same." He chuckled at his own humor. "Water would be appreciated, Tom."

I was out the door by the time he finished his reply, and in a few minutes returned with two paper cups of water. Bob drank them both before continuing to read.

"Those choosing to abuse their free will through suicidal means fail to realize that such action will remain forever on their consciousness - the one and only reality retained throughout eternity. Consciousness, along with free will are all that is taken with you when entering the unobstructed universe (Heaven, to those who prefer). Consciousness and free will must remain forever in harmony. Otherwise, both will be obstructions in an unobstructed universe, for a heavy consciousness weighs one down, and a 'too-free' free will destroys balance.

"The all-importance of consciousness is too often rationalized through abuse of free will. Freedom of speech, even thought, is your constitutional right. Respect it in keeping with your consciousness. Your existing laws allow freedom of choice to a point, but chose only what your conscience permits. The old adage: 'Let your conscience be your guide' still holds. However, should you feel that you are limited in answering a weighty question, go to a higher consciousness, one more evolved. But first, carefully analyze the question. Is it not self answerable? If so, it will prove that you have indeed evolved in spite of your doubts, even though a small scolding may have been required to make you believe in yourself.

"Think back, how many times have I told you that an answer to your needless question was not necessary and then smiled at your feeble attempt to not look embarrassed for having asked it. Your scolding was deserved, my smile was earned. Remember, I am very human!

"Reflect on my comment about expanding one's consciousness. Consider it valid, for both you and your consciousness are in evolution. I shall have more to say about the importance of consciousness as occasion warrants."

There was a long silence, while all three of us thought about Clair's words. Each of us, I guess, affected in a different way. Finally I said, "Tom, you said the second 20-year stretch after your 'remember-this dream' was an NDE without the black tunnel and the bright light. Is this a good time to explain?"

He looked at Bob, then at me. "I think it is. Remember I said there was no need for a black tunnel and the bright light, that other forces were involved?"

I nodded.

"And do you remember my story about the old man who lived to be 92 who had a very modern solution for his 17-year old daughter attracted to a married man?"

"I do. Never heard of a father inviting his daughter and her boy friend to move in with him. Happy ending, too." I was confused. "What's that got to do with an NDE?"

Tom's smile had disappeared. "A little background. Two of my long-time friends and academic colleagues were also friends and admirers of the old man with the problem daughter. I honestly don't know whether they knew about the episode I mentioned to you. But they knew the father well."

I guess I was showing a little impatience. "And the NDE?"

"That wise old man died in his sleep - precisely at the moment, six thousand miles away, I had a stroke. I wound up in the hospital for three weeks, double vision, couldn't walk. It was a bully stroke, Chris, but I survived and eventually got over my disabilities and within a year or so stopped taking any medication."

"No black tunnel or light?"

"No, Chris, but during the three weeks in the hospital, a second lighter stroke, and a major operation, I had absolute conviction I would make it. By then there was no doubt in my mind I still had much left undone on this earth. But even I was astounded by the strength of my conviction."

I wasn't getting his point.

"My two academic friends, separately and in confidence, told me it was no coincidence that the old man died at the precise moment of my stroke. Neither of the two of them had any interest in the psychic world and or had ever heard of an NDE."

"That's sure different from the kind I heard Pearl describe."

"There are many kinds. And remember, I had my Life's Review in a hospital in St. Cloud some years before that. They usually happen at the same time. Or, like Bob's experience, the Life's Review is omitted. I had the Life's Review first, and was guided through the gauntlets of two strokes and an operation, my two friends believe - and I do too - by the spiritual power of that man 92, his highly developed quality of consciousness."

I guess I was looking at him in a new way.

He shrugged. "However that may be, Chris, I've managed to do a lot of constructive work in the 20 years since then."

Bob had been listening quietly. "Tom, you told Chris some time ago, that I'd tell him more about J. B. Rhine's publication. I said he'd be more interested in what Rhine had researched but hadn't published. And you wanted me to mention that professor of philosophy who visited Duke University with the idea of 'exposing' Rhine."

Tom was nodding.

"Well," Bob continued, "Chris could only read the files of Dr. Rhine, since that fascinating account of his research has never been published. And you know the story of the philosophy professor better than I. You tell it."

I looked from one to the other. "Well, will one of you please tell me?"

Tom was laughing quietly. "It's really a funny story, Chris. This high-powered professor of philosophy from one of the three oldest universities in the country showed up one day at Dr. Rhine's office and said, 'Dr. Rhine, I'd like to examine your research files.'"

I was interested. "And?"

"Rhine not only said that was fine but offered to let the professor use the services of his assistant while he was at Duke. The Professor had said he would be there three weeks."

Tom seemed to be enjoying his story. "After three weeks, the philosophy professor came back to Dr. Rhine and explained that it was going to take longer than he had thought and asked to continue. Permission was granted, and the learned man went back to the files.

"After three months he came once again to Dr. Rhine and said that he was ready to return to his university, where he would write an extensive article that would expose the fallacies of Rhine's work. 'You see,' he said, "after more than 40 years of publishing extensively in the field of philosophy, I simply can't afford professionally to believe what I've seen.'"

I was astounded. "Who told you about it? Dr. Rhine?"

"No, the man he sent to our university to work with the plant pathologist. Dr. Rhine's assistant, who had been helping the professor of philosophy."

Chapter XXI

LIFE'S HARD TO FIGURE. That Friday, everything in my life seemed to turn upside down. I got the book I'd been waiting for. Some basic ideas were beginning to jell. I had decided Eve and I were going to begin seeing each other weekends.

When I got home Friday night, the letter was waiting. The hospital notified me that beginning on Monday my new schedule would be four p.m. to midnight, including Saturday and Sunday. Those hours meant hot traffic in emergencies. Days off Tuesday and Wednesday. The hospital had merged with a new HMO group.

There went Friday nights with Tom and Bob. Weekend dates with Eve.

Saturday morning, the phone rang about ten. It was Eve. Her first words were like a horse kicking you in the stomach. "Chris, the library has given me new hours. Eight-to-five, hour for lunch, off Saturdays and Sundays. We can have supper together without stealing time. And I'm free now on the weekends!"

For a month, I'd been working up the courage to ask Eve for regular weekend dates. I listened to her news, and just hung on to the phone kinda numb, wondering what the hell I'd done to deserve this.

Maybe it was that mind-reading streak of hers. I think she *heard* my frustration.

"Chris? No reaction. Anything wrong?"

I explained.

She waited a minute, then said, "Okay, we'll turn it around. Let's celebrate. Can I come over in about an hour to show you I can cook? You like Italian food?"

"Love it. Will you stay all day? . . . we can rent a video for Saturday night or go to a movie or just sit and talk . . . This is the last weekend I'll be free. Tuesday-Wednesday is my new weekend."

She hesitated for just an instant. "I'm really sorry about the new schedules. We'll figure it out. This is our first and last weekend for a while."

"Sorry? I'm mad! Maybe I'll look for another job."

"We'll talk about it. See you in an hour or so."

I moped around the little pad for two more hours, glancing at the book-on-loan, *The Unobstructed Universe*, without opening it. I couldn't wait for the doorbell to ring. When it did, I opened it fast and took Eve in my arms. The kiss was long and radiated up and down our bodies. The beginning of our first and last weekend - for how long?

I was still holding her after the kiss, and then noticed the bag of groceries in her arm that had been part of the hug. We laughed, and I took it from her and followed her into my kitchenette.

She lined up the Parmesan cheese, Tobasco sauce, tomatoes, celery, garlic, olive oil, green olives, number 9 pasta, Italian bread.

I grabbed the Romaine lettuce. "I know what to do with this - best Caesar salad this side of the Mexican border."

She clapped a hand over her mouth. "I forgot wine!"

It was my turn. With a big sweep of my arms I bent over to reach a cupboard and opened a small door. I pointed. "French, 1993, Bordeaux - for two years, saved for today!"

We spent a lazy afternoon cooking. Dinner began about five-thirty and went on with candlelight until nine. We ate a lot, drank the whole bottle, and by the time my desert was served (frozen Key lime pie again) we were both very mellow.

"Chris," Eve was looking at me through the candle flames, "I'm in love with you. Can you handle that?"

I knocked over the last of my wine, reaching for her. The embrace and kiss were long and searching. If there had ever been any doubt, it vanished. A reference librarian and a male nurse.

Neither of us a Tony or an Einstein. But we both were keenly aware of one another's quality - the quality of consciousness, as Bob would put it.

We were seated on the floor looking across a low coffee table. I got up and went around to her side of the table. We leaned against each other.

She looked at me a long time, then said quietly, "Let me hear you say it, so we'll both be sure."

We held hands, like two kids exploring the sense of touch. "I love you, Eve. And I AM! YOU ARE! And we're both in love with that reality. That's the only reality. We're not sure we can agree whether the wine was too dry or not dry enough. But we sure can agree that *you are* and *I am*. As our two old gentlemen put it, our *consciousness* is the one thing we can know for sure. And it's eternal - and evolving."

Eve said, "Let's talk about us, Chris. Who we are, where we're going, where we think we're going." She took a last sip of wine. "The new hours are lousy. But what we've found tonight is forever. Okay?"

The kiss was long, not burning with passion but warm with response. I couldn't believe that only this morning I was down at the bottom of the pit. And now, with Eve beside me, I was soaring - not looking down, *looking up!* My riddle was solved! Eve! There were two of us now, and that made us four times stronger than one of us. We had discovered one another. Thanks to the old prof and his musician buddy, we'd glimpsed an eternal future - like Bob's and Clair's.

I sat up straight and held Eve at arms length. "Eve, I learned so much since yesterday . . . I don't believe I'm living in the same world I was in two days ago."

Eve put a finger against my cheek. "Together," she said. "I am, you are - together *we are*. That's the one and only reality we can be sure of."

"Right now, with you in my arms and eternity as our future, I've got everything I can be sure of. I exit. You exit. WE EXIST! That's the one thing we know for sure. Maybe not much else - Einstein's theories or Tony's way of digging ditches. But I know I'm me, and you know you're you. Forever, I'm Chris. Forever, you're Eve. Nobody can change that. I like the idea. We'll manage the new hours. We can do it, now that we know we're real and forever."

She was looking at me, nodding the whole time I spoke. "Chris, we really found it. Each other and IT. For the first time, I think I understand that fuzzy word 'immortality." Right now, you and I are Chris and Eve. We can be sure of that. And the idea of filling out our quantity, our quantity of consciousness . . . I'm beginning to understand that, Chris. The two of us, working within the process of evolution. Together."

I was feeling expansive, probably encouraged by the wine. "I look forward to the next stage, Eve, so much so, I'll work like hell in this earthy plane, so I'm ready for the next step in evolution. Raising my quality to a higher degree. Like Tony in the next world becoming the boss of ditch diggers or me jumping from male nurse to director of research biology."

She gave me another squeeze. "Chris, I like you as a male nurse. That's who I fell in love with."

"I'm no Einstein. And not a Tony." I was getting the giggles. The wine, I guess. "Eve, I don't know who the hell I am - but *I am*. That's all I need to know to figure out what I was put on this earth to do. And when I know that, and I *will* know when I've found it, I'll do it better than anybody else. Because it's why I'm here."

Eve had caught my giggles. We both started laughing. I felt silly and finally managed to ask, "What's so funny?"

She struggled to keep from laughing, coughed, choked, and blurted out, "Your recipe for green mangoes. I found it." Her giggles came back. "Maybe I'll wind up a gourmet cook."

We sobered up and began eating our lime pie. It had thawed to just the right temperature, the same way Eve and I had thawed out all our reservations with one another. We both knew it. We belonged now. My riddle was solved!

Eve finished chewing a bite, wiped her mouth with a napkin, and said, "I'm thinking about Einstein. If I got the message straight, he's not only obliged to fulfill his quantity as full as possible with things like the fourth dimension, he's also got to lend a hand to the Tony's."

I thought about that. "Speaking of Einstein reminds me of Edison. Do you know he only slept four hours at a stretch - sometimes only a half-hour nap, when he was inventing?" Her look was a question. "What I mean is, big minds like Einstein's and Edison's don't require much sleep. They've got the extra time to help the Tonys."

The way she was looking at me I couldn't resist another quick kiss.

"Chris," she said, "helping the Tonys is something like holding that old man's wrist who was having stomach pains."

"You think it's that easy?"

"Every day we can do things like that . . . if we remember to . . . helping the Tonys has to be a habit. An every day habit. Little things to give somebody else a lift. A little extra push."

"You mean like a reference librarian sticking at it until she finds the recipe for green mangoes?"

This time she kissed me. The riddle of my baseball dream was solved.

Chapter XXII

EVE STAYED ALL night. I made breakfast the next morning, and we agreed that a walk was a good idea before washing the dishes. The air was pungent with the heady scent of Star Gazer lilies. My neighbor had a bed of them. It was balmy, but not humid like the day before. Dry, exhilarating, pumped you up with energy. Our pace was almost brisk, as though we knew where we were going and were enthusiastic not to lose any time getting there.

The late morning clouds, puffy white, scudded across the blue sky like a herd of albino buffaloes. We both had our eyes on the sky, holding hands, our thoughts running ahead of the clouds, faster than the wind. Eve and I kept looking up as we walked. Life was beautiful.

"Chris," Eve's focus came back to me, "what'll you do about Friday nights? I know they mean a lot to you."

I kissed her behind the ear. "I've been wondering about that too. I'm anxious to talk to Bob and Tom and see if they will change nights. Tuesday or Wednesday. Those two gentlemen - come to think of it, I don't know where they live or how they spend their time from one Friday night to the next."

Now there was a puzzle. Why had I never thought to ask them! I guess their exchange of experiences and whopping big thoughts from Clair filled my head so full, there was no room to think about other things. Maybe Tuesdays or Wednesdays would be okay. Maybe it didn't have to be at night. Maybe nine or ten some morning every week.

Eve glanced at me. "Phone number?

I stopped in my tracks. "Eve! I don't even know their last names, much less their phone numbers."

The more I thought about it the more anxious I became. They wouldn't be around until next Friday night. And I couldn't get off work on Friday nights. "Eve . . ." I guess she read my thoughts.

"Sure, Chris. I'll stick around until seven-thirty this coming Friday, get a phone number, and tell them what's happened . . . they'll work it out, Chris. I'm sure they'll accommodate your new schedule."

We walked on in silence, each of us, I guess, wondering about a solution to finding the right night for exchanging experiences. That was when I first got the idea of asking Eve to join us. "Eve, I have to talk to Tom and Bob, but wouldn't you like to join us?

It was out, before I remembered that she said she wasn't into these psychic things.

"Might be fun." Her smile and the sound of her laugh, like a springtime brook in the woods. "I'll bet it beats TV any night."

I remembered that for a while we had watched the news the night before, got disgusted with the Washington spin masters, and turned it off. "Sometimes," I was also remembering some of the surprises on Friday nights, experiences nobody could believe, unless it was happening to them, "sometimes, those Friday nights get exciting. Almost like learning there is a Santa Claus after all. But TV news - unless it's bad, you don't hear about it."

Eve said, "Last night, during the news, that breakthrough on cloning . . ."

"Yeah, we probably both had the same thought. How long before they try it on human beings?"

"The President said he won't let them."

"No, Eve, he said no federal funding for cloning human beings. He didn't mention that the first Amendment and free enterprise and eager mega-drug companies might produce somebody who would try."

Eve looked back up at the clouds. There was a smile on her face. "I'm not worried, Chris, about cloning human beings."

130

I waited for five steps, then counted to ten. "Eve," I said, "you mean you're not concerned that they might get around to cloning human beings?"

She gave me a strange look, as though she was surprised by my question. "Why concerned?"

I stopped walking. Wow! This gorgeous girl I thought I knew had thrown me for a loop. "Concerned! Suppose some genius figures out the way to produce a lot of little Einsteins. No more Tonys, or muddlers, like you and me, but only geniuses. Now that guy, whoever and whenever he manages the right formula, is going to be playing God." I shook my head and looked into her eyes. "Really, Eve, how can you say you're not concerned? Can you imagine what it would be like if the whole world was made up of only geniuses?"

The herd of sky buffaloes was forgotten. We walked on at a slower pace, each of us in our flights of thought, I guess, trying to imagine how that might be.

Finally Eve said, "I don't think it's because I'm Catholic . . . or because I'm not reading your psychic books . . . " She stopped again and looked at me. "Did you like the spaghetti I made last night?"

Well, I'm not too fast on the pick up. But a switch to spaghetti slammed the door shut in my face.

"Eve, really . . . yes . . . it was great . . ."

She looked disappointed. "Did you ever taste any spaghetti that good?"

I could see she was serious. I was also serious. I didn't even have to think. "No, Eve. Like I said last night. It was special . . . different . . . it was great! But, dear, we were talking about the possibility of cloning human beings. The switch to spaghetti's got me confused."

We started to walk again, and a glance at the sky showed me the albino buffaloes were nowhere in sight. Eve and I were in love. A reference librarian and a male nurse. She could read minds. If the words were too big, I had trouble even understanding the other guy's thoughts. Spaghetti and cloning. Okay, so I'm a dumb ass.

"Eve? Explain, please. Give me a hint. What's cloning human beings got to do with your spaghetti?"

Again she stopped walking. "My mother taught me to make spaghetti sauce, when I was about 15. I spent the next five years making the recipe my own. By now, I've had another ten years of practice. It *is* different, Chris, because I worked hard to make it special."

I nodded.

"No genius in a damn laboratory is going to figure out how to include that recipe in his cloning."

We were walking again. I reached for her hand.

"So. . .?"

"The experimenters are spending all their time on the *physical* requirements in cloning. If I were the mother stock - if that's the right word for the one being cloned - do you think for a minute that some genius who figures out how to clone human beings, with all his wizardry in the lab, will be able to figure out my recipe for spaghetti sauce?"

For the next few minutes we just swung along in silence. I was wrestling with Eve's recipe for spaghetti sauce. I guess she wondered why I was so dense. Maybe because I looked back up at the clouds again, I had a thought,. They had begun to look like "Dolly" the sheep. Then they began to change and looked more like a bunch of albino mice. Clones. Not Einsteins, not Tonys, not Eves, just a bunch of mice - who probably could never manage a recipe for Eve's spaghetti sauce. There was some sense to her reasoning, somewhere . . . I just couldn't get hold of it.

I laughed and kissed her on the nose. She liked that. "Next time I see Bob and Tom and Clair again, I'll ask them to explain why you shouldn't be concerned about someone cloning your spaghetti recipe."

Later in the day, when the dishes were done and we were thinking about an early supper, I fixed a tall summer drink for us. Eve made spicy dip. Not as good as her spaghetti sauce, but good. We went outside and sat on the steps. The air was still heady and set the mood for my thoughts about Eve.

Then she said, "Chris, about cloning . . ."

I shook my head and laughed. "Okay, Eve, I accept your theory about spaghetti sauce. I can't believe the problem is that simple."

"You mean that basic."

"Right! Basic! I have trouble thinking that cloning could be as basic as how to make good spaghetti sauce. Why not a bunch of geniuses - who don't know how to make spaghetti sauce - but do know how to do other things, like new theories of the atmosphere or the probability curve of meteorites hitting the earth or schemes for exploring black holes. Then suppose there's nobody around who knows how to dig ditches or change tires or pump gas."

"Or make special spaghetti sauce."

Eve was silent a moment. "Chris, I think my spaghetti recipe was a lousy way to try to convince you that cloning human beings is not that scary." She sipped her drink and dunked a tortilla chip into the dip. "Let me try something else."

I shrugged. Damn! I thought we had dropped that subject.

"Remember what you were telling me about consciousness? About the I AM, the only reality we can be sure of: *I EXIST*?"

I nodded.

"And you explained that our job, when we find it, is to do it better than anyone else. Use free will to do the job we were put on earth to do, *choose* to do it better than anyone else."

"I remember saying all that."

"And what did you say we were doing that was going to be essential to the evolution of our consciousness, when we get to the unobstructed half of the universe? Increasing the *quantity* of consciousness during this life in the obstructed half, so we could go on raising the *quality* of consciousness in the unobstructed half, right?"

"Right. Working on the how-muchness in this obstructed half of the universe."

"What about the *quality* of consciousness? The level of consciousness that makes one person a Tony and another one an Einstein to start with. Where does that come from?"

I thought about her question. If Tom and Bob and Clair had covered that question, I must have missed it. "Don't know, Eve. God-given, I guess." I suddenly realized I hadn't answered her question. "Okay, I don't know what I mean by that. Do you?"

"No, I don't.` But I'll bet your three psychic friends either know or can figure it out or will find out, if you ask them. And I'll bet you anything the answer has nothing to do with the wizardry of a scientific laboratory. How to clone a sheep or a mouse is the ultimate test of developing techniques to reproduce identical physical characteristics. But the quality of consciousness? The degree of consciousness that makes a Tony or an Einstein? No, Chris. I don't think the intellectual digging in the laboratory is ever going to figure that out. Nor figure out how to clone the quantity the mother clone has accumulated."

She was smiling mysteriously now. "That's why," she said slowly, "I want to join your group. To be sure my recipe is protected."

Chapter XXIII

TUESDAY AT 7:30 was the night selected by Bob and Tom, after Eve talked to them the next Friday night. When I showed up at the Park at seven, they weren't there. I waited 15 minutes, then went on to the library, arriving about 7:30. They were both sitting in their lounge chairs. Eve was in the one I usually occupy.

"Hi," I said, as though this was the normal meeting of the "exchanging-experiences club," now enlarged to include Eve, "howzit?"

Both men were cordial, but a little more distant than usual.

"Eve said you changed hours," Tom said, "so we didn't go to the Park but came directly here. Are you free to meet at the Park at seven?"

"Sure!" I found a straight-back chair. "I've got the whole day free. I'd hate to miss Bob's chat with the dogwood tree."

Eve spoke up. "He talks with a dogwood tree?"

I forced a smile. "Eve, I'll fill you in, now that you might belong to the club." Neither Bob nor Tom were smiling. So I asked, "I guess it's okay if Eve joins us?"

I felt Eve's eyes on me, but didn't look away from Tom. She was sitting very quiet, like a mouse, wondering which way to jump.

Bob answered. "Clair says there's better balance with a woman in our meetings."

Tom said nothing.

I nodded. "Great. With a foursome, sometime we might have to choose sides." The attempt at humor wasn't appreciated. Funny how the addition of one more person can change the balance of things. Even if number four was Eve.

It was Tom's turn. "Eve has been talking about cloning. Are you interested too?"

"Yes, I am. Neither of us know much about it. But we differ on how important it may be if it extends to human beings - eventually."

Without a smile Tom said, "Eve told us about her spaghetti recipe."

Now I didn't know where the hell I stood. "Oh," I said, waiting for the next shoe to drop.

Bob was smiling at Eve. "And we think she's on to something."

Now I did feel like an ass. First time in the club, first subject brought up, and my newcomer Eve was on to something. "Oh?"

Bob stirred in his chair and sat up straighter. "I think Clair's here now. I guess she was waiting for you, Chris."

After a pause, Bob went on, still his voice, but Clair's way of talking.. "Chris, you have a right to be concerned about the rapid development of cloning, especially some day, should it evolve to experimentation with human beings. You wonder if consideration is given to whether or not the *quality* of consciousness of the parent clone will be passed to another.

"Return to the words of Stephen in *The Unobstructed Universe*. He stated, and wisely so, that man is born, but his development is still limited to the extent of knowledge of the *wholeness* of evolution. Creators of clones would do well to understand that only half of evolution is known to them. Granted they should know or at least unconsciously recognize the truth of evolution's *quantitatve* development for mankind on earth. Examples of individual evolution abound. This is a fact well known by we who inhabit the unobstructed universe and strive to make it known in the minds of your men and women of science.

"Stephen refers to evolution as a law. He says that the whole of consciousness, the fundamental reality, is, therefore, in evolution. He maintains that the earth-bound or obstructed manifestations of consciousness are in evolution quantitatively only, and that the qualitative aspects of evolution, the second half, evolves only in the afterlife, where it is fully understood.[1]

"To date, earth science is ignorant of the important second half of evolution. Overlooked also is the fact that most, but not all, of mankind's inventions originate from the highly evolved minds of scientists in the unobstructed universe. They transmit their thoughts to the minds of researchers, knowingly or unknowingly receptive to them, in the obstructed half of the universe, where they are generally recognized as original thoughts and developments of earth-bound scientists engaged in basic research."

Tom broke in excitedly. "How many times I've heard men of science say, 'I had a hunch' or 'it came to me out of the blue.' These are the break-throughs in science awarded the Nobel Prize."

Bob, that is, Clair had waited patiently, then went on. "As more is learned about the truth of immortality, the quicker the gap between the two halves of the one universe will narrow. We in our phase of the one and only universe are working toward that end."

I was watching Eve. She seemed to be taking everything in stride, as though hearing thoughts from the other side was commonplace. I hoped she'd wait for one of the older gentlemen to speak She didn't.

"That feels right, Bob - I mean Clair - " Her confusion was momentary. "Our best scientists, whether working with their own ideas or hunches out of the blue, only recognize half of the evolution equation." She looked from Bob to Tom, then back again. "And those great men of science haven't the foggiest idea how to tap a person's lifetime of quantity - Chris and I call it 'how-muchness' - and for sure they're not aware of this business of *quality* and that *it* is what makes Tony Tony and Einstein Einstein."

Well, you've heard me admit to being slow. But this time I got it. I guess Eve was right. No need to be concerned about a lab full of scientists whose declared work place was developed like Harry Truman's Missouri philosophy, 'you gotta show me.' Then I remembered that those geniuses, Einstein included, who worked on the quantum theory were knowingly working with things that defied measurement and couldn't be seen. A quantum, smallest unit of energy. Through a glass darkly? It was getting a little lighter.

---

[1] see further *The U.U.*, pp. 90-92.

I could see from Bob's face that Clair was still there.

His voice suddenly continued. "I have stressed the importance of need to accept the truth of immortality. Acceptance of this fact continues to grow.

"Look about you today. Motion pictures, TV series, books, magazines, and newspapers are revealing an increasing openness to the concept of life after death. In times past, brief flames of interest in life's continuations occurred, but there was nothing like the burgeoning interest today. It continues to grow, even among some circles that previously denied such a possibility. Immortality is becoming a household word.

"Our work now in progress [that of Bob, Tom, and Clair] is an excellent example of promulgating the reality of life's continuation. It is directed especially to the attention of previous hold-outs who have been defending their rigid stand of denial, often in the name of science. Some are becoming more flexible in their attitude simply because they, too, inwardly wish that they might be given an opportunity to continue their valuable work in a life hereafter."

It felt to me like it was time for a break. Not for coffee, but to be sure we had pulled things together. "Mind if I try to state what I think all this is about?" I looked first at Bob, then at Tom. I knew I didn't have to look at Eve. "I think I understood the fine print. But I wanna be sure. Okay?"

Everybody nodded.

"If I've got it right, we don't need to worry about cloning, because no one has any idea how to clone either the quality or the quantity of consciousness. Most scientists, in fact, probably don't even know such a thing exits. In other words, if they use an Einstein as a parent clone, they'll get someone who's going to grow up to have a thick, bushy head of hair and a mustache. But whether he'll have an Einstein or a Tony quality of consciousness - or something in between - they have no idea. The idea of the quality of a person, their degree of development as an I AM, has never found its way to the science lab. Experiments, I guess, are headed in a different direction. The same goes for the quantity of consciousness, the how-muchness an Einstein or a Tony or someone in between developed up to the time he or she was cloned. I guess I'm agreeing with Eve. No need to worry about Eve's recipe."

That was the first long speech I'd ever made in our exchanges of experience. It was probably Eve's presence that gave me the courage. I was a little nervous, now that it was all out.

"Well, done!" Bob reached over and patted me on the shoulder.

"You've got it," Tom said.

Eve said nothing, but her eyes said all I was waiting for.

Chapter XXIV

THE NEXT DAY, WEDNESDAY, I took Eve to lunch. We had a quick one at the Greek's, a salad loaded with big black olives and feta cheese. I bought a bag of Nacho cheese crackers from the machine, then headed for the Park. I wanted to show Eve those two dogwood trees.

When we got there, I threw some crackers out for the pigeons. I can't talk to trees and flowers like Bob or to animals like Tom's grandfather, but I could tell the way those pigeons pecked at the crackers, hesitated, then pecked some more, they liked the plain ones better. Eve was watching me, as I threw out a few more.

"You always bring crackers for the pigeons?"

"Unless I forget. Not Nacho, just plain ones. They like them better, but the Greek's only had Nacho."

For about five minutes, we sat on a bench, feeding the birds. I saw Eve glance at her watch. "Guess we'd better start back."

I pointed to the two dogwood trees. "That's the tree Bob talks to."

We walked over to examine it, and I showed her how that dogwood had grown faster and better than the other one, the one Bob didn't talk to.

She didn't say anything, only smiled and said again, "We'd better start back."

As we made our way toward the library, I said, "Well, Eve, what did you think about Bob's dogwood compared to the other one?"

After three or four paces, she said, "Bigger leaves, healthier trunk, altogether much more vigorous growth."

"That's what talking to it does."

"How do you know?"

"What do you mean, how do I know! You just saw for yourself the difference."

After a few more paces, she said, "Did he take soil samples? They're more than 20 feet apart. When they tore up the ground making this Park, maybe Bob's dogwood got planted in better soil."

Now that's a woman for you. I had everything all settled in my mind about Bob talking to trees, and now Eve shoots it down.

"I'll ask him, Eve. He'll be impressed that you challenged him."

For another block we were silent. Then I asked, "Well, what did you think about last night? Think your recipe's safe for posterity?"

She looked into my eyes as we kept walking. "Look, Chris, I'm in love with you. And one thing you can count on: I'll always be honest - almost always. Anyhow, whether what we heard really came from Clair or was just the old professor's mind speaking, whatever - the message was loud and clear. And strong. I thought about it half the night, instead of sleeping. And I woke up rested and feeling fine."

I debated whether to try to explain evidential to Eve. About how floored Pearl had been when the Ouiji board told us something she had kept secret from me. The identity of her friend - her sister - who rushed too fast in beginning psychic work. I thought about the differences in the way phrases were strung together by Clair and certain words she used that simply weren't Bob's way of talking. I was remembering Bob's sorta stuffy style of speech, like the professor he was, holding forth. Clair's talk sounded more like a messenger from the unobstructed universe - but it was still personal.

Evidential. Wanting to be convinced. "Eve, I hope you won't be offended as a reference librarian, if I recommend a couple of books for you to read."

She gave me a funny look. "Psychic stuff, I suppose."

"Easy reading. Helps you understand something called 'evidential.'" I mentioned *Our Unseen Guest, The Betty Book*, and a couple of others.

We had reached the steps leading up to the automatic doors of the library. I embraced Eve, felt my temperature rise after a long kiss, and said, "How about a date next Friday at midnight? I don't have to work until four p.m. on Saturday, and you've got Saturday off. Okay?"

"I'll be waiting for you at the hospital, Friday at midnight." She gave me another kiss and turned and ran up the steps.

"Wait inside," I called after her. "Sometimes some strange ones hang around outside."

I turned to go, when I saw someone at the top of the stairs waving to me. It was Tom!

I ran up the steps. "How nice to bump into you, Tom. Almost like the time we met in a bar, seated on adjacent stools."

"This time, maybe not as mysterious. We were told you had taken Eve to lunch. We knew when you'd be back. Bob's got another nudge from Clair, the seminar room's free. We'll explain to Eve next Tuesday night."

Inside the seminar room there sat Bob in his lounge chair, a big smile on his face. "I think your new schedule's going to work out just fine."

He went on talking, while Tom and I found chairs. "Did Eve say anything about her first evening with us?"

I squirmed a little as I sat down in my chair. Dear old Bob. Did I dare tell him what Eve had said . . . about the dogwood and even Clair's message?"

"She did. She said the message was loud and clear . . . and strong. It kept her awake half the night. But she got up feeling rested."

Tom spoke up. "The librarian said you were headed toward the Park Did you show her Bob's dogwood?"

"Oh, yes . . . she was impressed with its growth compared to the other dogwood."

Bob asked. "Is that all she said?"

Well, there it was. Lie or hurt the old man's feelings! "Well . . ." I couldn't outright lie to Bob; maybe I could soften it.

143

"Eve had a question about the soil. But I couldn't tell her anything."

I swear Bob's eyes were sparkling. "Eve's a mighty sharp little girl. When you have your next date with her, tell her I had comparative core samples of the soil run in the university lab before I started talking to the tree. Both soils are precisely the same, even the relative moisture content."

Have you ever thought you were about to be caught in a lie, then suddenly find out you didn't have to fib? I felt like kissing old Bob. Instead I said, "I'm seeing her Friday night at midnight. I'll tell her."

"Anything else?"

"You mean, Eve? Did she say anything else about last night?"

Bob was nodding. "I thought it might have troubled her that Clair was using my voice. Not a very conspicuous demonstration of communication by my wife. Little by little we'll try to acquaint Eve with evidential. We want her to be sure she knows that Tom and Clair and I are convinced she's an important addition to the team."

So the old man had got the message and saved me from a fib. I guess one of the reasons he liked Eve was they could both do a little mind reading.

Bob's face had grown serious. I knew Clair was about to begin.

"Free will is your right. Exercise it freely, but not before balancing it against the counterweight of conscience. Free will and conscience must remain in balance.

"Temptation and the freedom to indulge it swing the pendulum of balance away from conscience to such extent that temptation begins to dominate, leaving but shreds of conscience to counter it. Hence the old adage: 'He doesn't have a shred of conscience left.' Sparse though it may be, enough conscience remains to encourage continued growth. New beginnings stemming from reclaimed conscience may arise from earlier pain of self-incrimination - realization that there is no one to blame for one's faults other than self. That alone is enough to help re-balance an out-of-balance scale of one's conscience."

Bob paused, and I took the break as a chance to ask a question. "I'm getting a little confused, Bob - Clair - you've been talking about conscience. I guess we've all had a guilty conscience about one thing or another. So I know what that is. But how does 'conscience' relate to that other big thought you use frequently, *consciousness?*"

"The quality of consciousness, the I AM," Clair continued, "in contrast to conscience, is *fixed* and exists individually in degrees. Conscience, on the other hand, also exists in degrees, but it is *not* fixed. Plumbing its depth, understanding the process of its development also proceeds in degrees. For example, to dip into the *shallows* of conscience, to appease what might otherwise be disallowed by deeper conscience - that is rationalization, a sub-surface wetting, cleansing oneself of something dishonest. Shallowness is best recognized by the person who wades in it."

The quick glance among Bob, Tom, and me was a clear sign that each of us remembered the weakness of rationalizing.

"The reality of conscience," she went on, "should never be underestimated. It's the real identity of self, when graduating to the unobstructed universe. Only you can judge your status, based on the content of your conscience.

"Self-evaluation in your review of life. Judging oneself is better accepted than being judged by another. You alone know how much or how little effort you have given toward the cleansing of conscience in preparation for graduation, bearing in mind that a conscience soiled is immediately recognized by a higher consciousness. Be aware of that before mingling in the company of higher degrees of consciousness that make up the unobstructed universe."

I looked at Tom. He was looking at Bob. Bob was looking at me. The presence in the room could be felt. For the first time, I was aware of Clair's presence.

"Bob," I said, "if I understand what Clair's been saying, I'd like to say it again in my own words, to be sure I got it. All of it seems to me new and very important."

Bob nodded but said nothing.

"Clair has informed us," I said, "that in addition to things learned earlier - like finding the job we were put on earth to do, doing it with our best effort to increase our quantity, our how-muchness of consciousness - in addition we have to keep a careful balance between free will and conscience. We all know what a conscience is. And we sure know what temptation is that sometimes bothers our conscience. The big news is, when that moment comes - out of the black tunnel and into the light - a soiled conscience is immediately recognized. She told us that we're the best judge of how well we've managed to balance free will and conscience, a judgment we make at the time of our life's review. If I get it right, we're the ones who can make sure we graduate with flying colors."

Chapter XXV

FRIDAY AT MIDNIGHT, I found Eve waiting for me just inside the double doors of the hospital. We embraced and kissed hurriedly. I grabbed her hand and pushed through the swinging doors. "Let's get out of here! Friday accidents. They keep coming in."

She knew I was upset. I could tell the way she squeezed my hand. "Pretty bad?"

I shook my head. "Eve, if everybody who drinks could spend Friday night with me, they'd quit drinking. Torn up teenagers . . . over-dressed baby boomers in their fast BMWs . . . old folks who shouldn't still have a driver's license."

The squeeze got stronger.

"Chris . . ." The voice was loud behind us. It was Pearl.

I turned around. "Hi, Pearl."

"Jeez, what a night! Will you and your girl walk me down to the bus stop? It gets kinda scary at this hour."

"This is Eve. Pearl pulls the midnight shift once a week."

The two ladies probably smiled in the dark. It was hard to see.

"Hi, Eve. We talked on the phone once."

She fell in step between me and Eve and put a hand on my shoulder, kinda like she needed support. I hadn't had a chance to talk to Pearl for several weeks. She sounded lonely.

"Rough night for nurses, male and female," I said.

147

Pearl dropped her hand from my shoulder, as though she suddenly realized it was there. "I hate Friday nights to work."

Eve looked past me at Pearl. "Chris and I are going to have a midnight cocktail. Join us?"

"I don't wanna bust in on your date."

I insisted. The three of us found a bar.

We sat in a booth, Eve and I on one side, Pearl on the other. "You two going steady?"

Eve's beautiful laugh brought a smile to Pearl's face. "No one has ask us that before. Yes, I guess so, if you mean not going out with anyone else."

Pearl's smile became a grin. "He's kinda rough around the edges, but otherwise a helluva nice guy."

"I know . . . and I like the rough edges."

It's no fun to be appraised by two females, even though I liked them both - in very different ways, of course. "Pearl," I said to Eve, "is the girl who keeps me from quitting my job. She's got that special kind of nursing grit. It guarantees that if it needs doing, she'll do it."

"See what I mean? Rough around the edges."

We ordered tall drinks. "Pearl, have you been doing any more reading or automatic writing?"

I saw her shoot a quick glance at Eve. "He got you hooked too?"

Eve's answer was as quick. "I'm still on the rough edges."

Pearl downed half her drink. "Naw, I quit. Begin to sound like I was talking to myself."

I looked her in the eye. "Mebbe that's the problem. Nobody to talk with about things like this. Pearl, my fault. I should keep closer track of what you do in your spare time."

Pearl's laugh was loud, not quite a cackle. "You got enough to think about." She was looking at Eve. "I've been doing some more reading. About NDEs. I didn't know they're so common."

I said, "Mebbe not common, Pearl, but not too rare either, now that people aren't afraid to talk about it. I get the feeling that an NDEs becoming like membership in a club."

"The one's I've seen weren't the kind of club I wanna join."

Eve's black eyes flashed at Pearl. "I've read a little about them. There are many kinds. And I've got the impression that it's

148

not a matter of being invited to join a club. If you need it and it's the right time to help you learn something, you might get lucky and experience the NDE." She looked at me. "I've been learning from Chris and his two friends that experience - exchanging experiences- is a great teacher."

Pearl finished her drink. "Okay, you two love birds. I can make it to the bus stop from here. Nice to put a face with that voice, Eve. See you around." And she was out of the booth and on her way to the exit.

Eve watched her go. "Hang on to that friendship, Chris. She's the rock of Gibraltar. Somebody there when you need her." She looked into my eyes. "But she needs somebody, too, Chris. Take her out for lunch some Tuesday or Wednesday."

"I'll try to remember, along with your phone number and Tuesday night meetings - and a lot of heavy reading still ahead."

I was wondering whether next Tuesday I could bring a brown bag lunch for Pearl and me to eat in the rose garden.

Sunday afternoon I took Eve by subway and bus to U Mass Boston, and we walked over to my favorite spot near the JFK Memorial Library. In the distance the waves were choppy, the breeze was strong enough to blow your hat off, if you wore one.

We sat on the grass and held hands, looking at a couple of brave boats running before the wind. The clouds were thin and moving fast. No Rorhshock patterns today, just a thin veil sliding fast through the sky. I wondered how, if Eve and I could ride along on that slithering sky cover, how things would look, here on earth.

"Have you been working on your baseball dream, Chris?"

The question startled me for a moment. "No . . . I haven't even thought about it."

"Not even the riddle? How I got into it?"

"We solved that one!" I looked at her I-know-something-you-don't-know smile. "You have any ideas about the rest?"

She shook her head, and I couldn't tell whether it was because she didn't have any ideas or because, like Tom, she thought it was something I was supposed to work out.

"You think I'll have to wait until I'm 60 or 80 or 100 to find the answer to the dream?"

That special smile was still there. "I think you'll find out when you least expect it. It hasn't anything to do with a cycle of 20 years." She put a finger against my lips, as I was about to speak. "I know about Tom's dream. But you're Chris. Different dream, different I AM, different time cycle." She looked out to the sea. "I'll be working on it with you, Chris. It won't take us too long."

Chapter XXVI

I DIDN'T HAVE a chance to talk to Eve again until the following Tuesday night, after we all met in the seminar room. When Bob, Tom, and I got to the library, Eve was waiting for us. She was in my chair again. So I pulled up the straight-back. We only kissed with the eyes, but that was enough.

Bob patted Eve on the hand. "You want to know more about evidential. Tom and I think an experience of his might be pertinent."

Tom's smile and the light in his eyes looked like an interesting experience was coming up. "I have to start with a little background. Before the United States got involved in World War II, I got a clerk's job in an aircraft plant. A lot of self-study in the metal shops and some midnight oil landed me a promotion to the job of 'beginning tool planner.' After five years and several aircraft companies later, I had become a 'trouble shooter' and a class 'A' tooling engineer.

"The last two of those years was when I got to know Bob." He looked over at Bob, as though to confirm what he was saying. "In the beginning of our friendship, I told him about a new interest I'd found in books like *Our Unseen Guest* and *The Betty Books*. His training as a university scientist gave our talks a needed balance. And one more bit of background - his first wife was one of the most gifted psychic mediums I've ever known."

151

I guess my mouth was open in surprise. But he had made it clear that Clair was Bob's second wife. Well, whatever experience was in Tom's mind, it wouldn't be dull.

"Early in 1944," Tom continued, "I thought my draft number would be coming up. So I went to a Navy recruiting office to sign on. They said they'd check with my draft board and that my aircraft record would probably qualify me for Lieutenant J.G. - Junior Grade. Now comes the beginning of the experience Bob wanted Eve to hear."

Eve was sitting up straight, not missing a word or facial expression, as Tom proceeded.

"One night at Bob's house I was full of questions about my immediate future. Neither of us were yet very experienced in the psychic world, so we hadn't learned to avoid questions. When I told Bob I was waiting to hear from the Navy and what they had told me, he suggested we see whether his wife could get answers to some of my questions." Tom grinned at Bob. "Today, we know better."

Bob cleared his throat a couple of times and nodded. "That was long ago, Tom."

"Anyhow, his wife agreed to go into trance, her usual mode of reception in a type of communication known as 'direct voice.' Another voice taking over the psychic medium - sometimes a woman, sometimes a man, once in a while in a foreign language she didn't know. Communication was never in her own voice."

My glance at Eve confirmed she was all ears.

"I don't remember exactly how the questions began, but the voice responded at once with the startling announcement, 'you will be in the Army Infantry.' Well, I had already told Bob about the Navy. So, we just looked at one another and shrugged. It was understood that we should never appear to invalidate information being received."

Tom was silent for a moment, reflecting, I guess, on how to shorten his tale. "Then I asked what I'd be doing in the Army Infantry. 'Writing history,' was the answer. I questioned - and probably shouldn't have - how I could get a writing job so late in the war. 'A special program will be created,' was the immediate response."

Well, Tom was doing a good job with his tale, but he had me squirming with what we were hearing. The guy was all but

152

signed up with the Navy, and this trance medium kept on talking about the Army!

"I guess Bob and I were almost indifferent to the responses by then, because all the answers sounded like somebody's invention and a rationalization to justify it. Maybe it was a trouble maker on the line Anyhow, I thought I'd try one last question. Like anyone facing the service, I wondered whether I'd live through it. So I asked something like, 'How will I leave the Service?' The answer was prompt. 'Hospitalized for Shell Shock - Medical discharge."

Eve spoke up. "And did you wind up in the Navy? A Lieutenant Junior Grade?"

Tom smiled. "My draft board informed me that I was essential to the aircraft industry. So, I went on working for the aircraft company, trouble shooting in the problems of tooling design. Actually I was feeling good about everything. I guess I was happy to learn that my job counted. Three month later, I was drafted into the Army Infantry."

Tom was no longer focused on any of us in the room. He seemed to be seeing things that once had been. "My basic training for the South Pacific was cut short by the Belgian Bulge. I shipped out to the European front. There were some unforgettable times, when the old Queen Elizabeth was dodging a fast submarine, when we were listing 32 degrees, or pitching about in an LST trying to cross a choppy English Channel."

He laughed. "In fact, we lay at anchor in the middle of the Channel all night, riding out a storm. A landing on the beach from the mouth of the LST, a long hike up a hill, with a pack and equipment that outweighed me by four pounds. A rainy night in a tented camp, where the water was half way up the legs of the cot. Then came a couple of days on the famous 40-and-eight box cars of World War I, followed by a few days in a replacement depot. Then I was assigned to a blacked-out Division, spearheading the invasion of Germany heading east from the Rhine river.

"On my way to a fox hole I was pulled off a truck and taken to Division Headquarters, where a Major questioned me about my brief writing career. The Major was the Division Historian who wrote 'After-after Action Reports' while the Division was engaged with the enemy. SHEAF didn't like his style of reports; he spotted my modest credentials as a writer, and suddenly I belonged to

Division Headquarters, where I joined 10 enlisted men in G-3, as the new Division Historian-without-title."

For a moment Tom was silent. "The 10 enlisted men were envied by the other 35,000 soldiers in the Division, because they worked in the War Room and knew where we were headed and when we'd jump off for the next engagement. It was a heady responsibility, knowing everything the General Staff knew and remembering never to utter a word to anyone outside the War Room.

"We weren't safer than any of the other soldiers. In fact, we were the nerve center of the Division. Headquarters Forward was a constant target for bombing, strafing, frog-men, tank drives. Soon I realized that other enlisted personnel in the Division understood that we in G-3, combat and training, were sworn to silence. But a new face in the War Room had to be tested for the first month or so. Finally they let me alone. It was a very special job."

He glanced up at Bob. "There was a non-stop drive from the Rhine River to the Elbe River, 30 kilometers from Berlin. And in the month of April, during that drive across Germany, my Division History - the After-after Action Report - was nearly 80,000 words long. I've never had what Bob experienced as an NDE - but in that drive there were quite a few experiences near death.

"By now I realized Bob's wife was right again. I not only landed in the Army Infantry but also wound up writing Division history. The opening in Division Headquarters for one more enlisted man was made possible, because a new program had been created in anticipation of V-E day. More personnel was needed to continue educational training for G.I.s, who'd have to wait their turn for transportation to bring them home. Five months after VE Day, I had a medical discharge from the Army for 'Battle Fatigue.'"

I stared at Eve, Eve was staring at Tom. Bob was looking at me. Wow! I could see she was as impressed as I was. But her question startled me.

"Fascinating, Tom. You have some kind of proof of all that?"

I swallowed hard. She was going to get kicked out of our club before she really knew what it was about.

154

Tom looked at Bob. "After I became the substitute Division Historian, I sent Bob a letter. I think he still has it." Bob was nodding. "Of course he already had learned I was in the Army and not the Navy. My medical discharge is a matter of record. But Eve, you're right to ask the question."

It was my turn to speak up. "Tom, that's as good as your 60-year old dream."

"If you remember the parts I've already told you about - things that happened after the War - it's really just an early part of working my way through a dream that happened when I was 19."

Eve was looking at me.

"I'll fill that in later," I told her.

For a few minutes, nobody spoke. Then Tom said, "Bob and I haven't felt the need of 'evidential' for a long time. It becomes more unbelievable not to believe than to accept the fact that we're in touch with others from the unobstructed universe. I admit it's reassuring, now and then, when Clair tucks in a little 'evidential.' It's a reminder that we're headed in the right direction." He was looking at Eve intently. "You won't be convinced about evidential, until something of the kind happens to you."

Bob was clearing his throat and stirring around in his chair, a sure sign something was on his mind. "Eve, I just had a little nudge from Clair. She says your sister's going to be okay. Does that make any sense? I didn't know you had a sister. Has she been ill?"

Eve shot a glance my direction. I knew what she was thinking, that I had told Bob and Tom about her kid sister and her problem with drugs. With my eyes and a shake of my head I tried to reassure her.

Eve turned her head away from me. She was quite still, very calm. I guess I'd say "chilly." She looked from Bob to Tom, but not at me. "My kid sister had a little period of depression," she said, "but tell Clair 'thanks,' Sis is okay now."

I was about to suggest a coffee break, thinking I could try to make Eve believe I had never mentioned her sister to anyone, when one of the librarians from the Main Desk entered the Seminar room. "Are you Chris? A lady on the phone says she's a friend of yours and that it's urgent you come to the phone."

155

I got up at once, wondering who the hell knew about my Tuesday night meetings in the Seminar Room. Pearl! Pearl was the only one. I began walking a little faster.

On the phone she came right to the point. "Chris, I had to work Emergency again tonight. Too many called in sick . . . Chris, your girl Eve, her sister. She's been in an accident. Boy friend high on coke. The Doc's finished sewing up her leg. She's gonna be okay, tell Eve. Maybe later she'll want some plastic surgery."

I guess I thanked her for the call. I was numb stumbling back to the Seminar Room. Eve's sister! Damn! Some kinds of evidential can be hard to take.

Chapter XXVII

THE FOLLOWING WEEK, I met Eve's sister Joan, and talked with the doctor about the accident. Six hours after the accident, the boy driving died of a head injuries. Except for a badly mangled left leg and constant sedation, Joan was all right. It was a miracle. The car was so badly twisted from going over a concrete wall and into a brick causeway, it had to be pried apart to get her out.

I was impressed with Eve. "Stoic," is the word.

It was Tuesday again, and we both went to the park. Tom and Bob were already there, so we started out at once for the library. I had acquired the old gentlemen's phone number - they shared a bachelor apartment - and had called them about Eve's sister.

Eve spoke to them as we walked. "Joan came home yesterday, and the doctor said she should work with a walker a little bit every day." She bit her lip. "Joan's a very beautiful girl . . . except for what happened to her left leg. She won't want to go to the beach any more."

We were holding hands as we walked. I gave a squeeze. "The doc said she could have plastic surgery in a few months."

Eve shook her head. "We talked about it. After that experience on the operating table, she's changed. She said it was a strong lesson. The accident. She thinks what happened gives her a second chance. It will help her grow up. Joan said, 'No plastic surgery. Not now . . . in case I need a reminder of what I used to be. Maybe when I've become a new me.'"

As we walked, Bob asked, "What was the experience on the operating table?"

I squeezed Eve's hand again and heard her say evenly, "Joan had what you call a Near Death Experience."

Bob was nodding, and I couldn't help but wonder, if Clair had already told him about it. "Did she describe it to you?"

"She did. In detail. The blackness, not exactly a tunnel, but for a long time there was blackness. Then she saw this glow ahead. And as she moved toward it, the light became brighter - but not harsh, Joan said, just warm and beautiful with a lot of colors. She said she felt at peace."

Bob was listening intently. "And then?"

"The next thing she became aware of was the doctor's voice saying, 'That was a sonuvabitch! If there had been another few minutes before we got her on the table . . . anyhow, she's going to be okay.'"

We had the Seminar Room to ourselves. I didn't even look as Eve sat in my usual lounge chair, just pulled up the straight-back.

Bob began by assuring Eve that Joan's Near Death Experience was becoming quite common. He explained that similar experiences, different in detail, had been reported widely, and that those who experienced an NDE, even the few that were not entirely pleasant, felt it had changed their lives.[1] They no longer feared death. And they knew they had been given another chance to develop their quantity of consciousness.

Some of this she had heard from me.

Bob was clearing his throat again. Feeling a little impish and probably too bold I said, "Bob, is Clair waiting in the wings?"

He gave me a wink and nodded. "Yes, I think she's got something she'd like to pass along."

Once more he cleared his throat, then proceeded to speak. "There still exists a fear of death, though recent accounts of NDEs are removing much of it. As more accounts and variations of them are brought to attention, fear of death lessens. Many who cling to

---

[1] For a general summary of common reactions see further Jean Ritchie, *Death's Door*, 1994, pp.20-26; and cf. Chapter 16.

their original fear are beginning to wonder as more is learned about the personal experiences of those who have touched death and returned to tell of its wonder.

"Consider the difference between death and birth. During the birthing process the fetus undergoes a frightening experience, in many cases, physical abuse. The fetus is moved from the comfort of its womb to the birth canal, which, in part, resembles a dark tunnel. Often the fetus is subject to rough jostling to keep it moving, sometimes to the brutal push-pull of special instruments required to assure delivery. It is then suddenly exposed to blinding, artificial lights, grabbed, turned upside down, and severely swatted on the buttock to initiate breathing - all of this accompanied by the loud sounds of 'ohs' and 'ahs' of strange voices. Small wonder the new-born finds solace when finally laid on the warm abdomen of the mother - the nearest thing to being back in the womb."

Well, that was something to think about! Death is easier than birth. We don't remember the experience of birth, even though the mother does and sometimes even describes it. But the thought that it's easier, more pleasant to die than to be born . . . huh! that was a twist. The many reports of a kind of euphoria in the course of an NDE, and now this description of rough handling at the time of birth.

Eve said, looking at Bob "I told Joan about you and Tom - and Clair. And about the new thoughts that are really new forms of some old thoughts." She paused, pulled a handkerchief from her pocket and blew her nose. "Joan's changed. If I had told her that a few weeks ago, she'd have laughed in my face. Now she just listens, nods, and says, 'That sounds right.'" She reached over and laid a hand on Bob's arm. "Do you think she should do some reading - about all these things you talk about?"

Bob shook his head. "Not now. Let her recuperate in the warmth and security of her NDE. I think she realizes she's joined the privileged few. Give her a while. She'll ask about books later."

"She's got music," Eve said. "This accident won't interfere with that."

"Is she a performer?" Tom was curious.

"Viola and guitar. She plays well, but her real interest is writing music."

"What kind?"

"Songs, mostly. The kids she runs around with think she's good. Most of the songs are over my head."

"How?"

"Not the tune. The text." Eve shook her head. "Some of them I just don't get. But her friends think she's great."

Tom had turned his attention to Eve. He moved his chair, so that it faced her. "Ever talk with her about the creative process?"

Eve laughed. "No! I wouldn't know how to begin."

Tom had a mysterious smile. "Can I give you a couple of hints? She might understand."

"Sounds a little far out, to me."

"It is. I'm no longer sure how much of this is from reading, how much from experiencing, how much from just knowing, learned in the course of what I sometimes call 'direct.' Not a voice. Not even worded thoughts. But a kind of implosion of *just knowing*." He paused and looked at Eve and then me. "The word 'noetic.' Ever hear of it?"

When we shook our heads, he just nodded.

I could see it was going to be difficult to hang on to this discussion. If it wasn't too tough to understand, if *I* could get it, then it might be something Joan would understand.

"Creativity," Tom said, "comes from a constant stream of energy. It's the source for poets, writers, musicians, actors, composers, song writers, hand weavers, potters, sculptors, painters - that long list of creative people, all ages, who are constantly involved with the creative process. Even when they're not creating."

Eve looked at me for help. I needed it myself.

She looked back at Tom. "I don't get it. You mean they're creating when they're not creating?"

"Let's say, when they're not conscious of creating. Let's go back to that first idea. Creativity is like a river or current of energy. The song writer or the sculptor dips into that stream and 'arrests,' that is, stops or isolates a glob of that creative energy, still unformed but vibrant with energy. In bursts of complementary energy, 'matching' energy - let's say, the same 'frequency,' whatever I may mean by that - the song writer or the sculptor creates, little-by-little, until, with constant critical revision a song or a sculpture comes into existence. It, the new song, the sculpture, also, represent a source of creative energy."

I took a deep breath. "I was with you, until that last thought. You mean the new song is part of the same big stream of creative energy?"

"Yes! You've got the idea. Everything created contributes to the process of creativity. Its energy, the new song, returns some of its energy to the main stream, where it may contribute, the next time around, to a new dance or an aria performed in Lascala or a poem."

I looked at Eve and she at me.

"Thanks, Tom. I'll try it on Joan. There's more to hear, right?"

He grinned. "Yes, Eve, a lot more."

Without understanding why, I knew for sure this was something Joan would grab on to. Her wave length. Her new frequency.

Chapter XXVIII

PEARL WAS WAITING for me at midnight the next Saturday, when I got off work. She was standing just outside the swinging doors of the hospital. I made it clear I was surprised.

"Pearl, you got nothing better to do than stick around this place on Saturday night till midnight? Christ! this is probably the worst night in the week. Join me in a beer - or something stronger?"

She looked worn out. "Yeah. Something stronger."

We didn't talk much until we were in the closest bar, and I had ordered two Wild Turkeys on the rocks. Expensive, but what the hell! First drinking date I'd had with Pearl in a long time. Since our talk in the Rose Garden.

"You pretty serious about Eve?"

Our drinks arrived, and we clicked glasses in an undeclared toast to ourselves.

"I guess so. Yeah. For sure. Eve and I have something going."

There was a long silence, while we took a few more sips of Wild Turkey. Pearl looked bushed. I wondered what the trouble was and how I could help.

"Chris . . ."

Here it came.

"You remember the trouble my sister had and went to a psychiatrist?"

I nodded.

"Same problem, only this time it's me."

I looked at her. "Under psychiatric treatment? Seeing a shrink regularly?"

She gave me a funny look and smiled. "You know, Chris, when I hear you put it that way, I don't think I need one. No, I haven't started yet. But . . . I keep hearing voices. No Ouiji board, no automatic writing. But I'm hearing voices."

I wasn't sure of my next line. But I tried. "Pearl, St. Joan of Arc heard voices."

She finished her drink, I finished mine and ordered two more. We didn't speak again until the drinks arrived. She took the lead.

"Look, Chris. I know you got problems of your own. Everybody has. But honestly I don't know who else to talk with."

I assured her I was glad to help if I could.

"I know, you got your hands full with Eve, and now her sister with an NDE."

"You know about that?"

"Half the hospital knows about it. She was very verbal during surgery. Word gets around. Chris . . ."

She paused for a healthy swig of Wild Turkey. "A lot of nurses and some interns are beginning to buzz about it."

It was my turn to try the second drink. "Pearl, you're talking to a beginner. I still don't know much about this psychic business."

"I thought Eve got that book for you, *The Unobstructed Universe*."

"She did. And I've been reading it. Trying to read it. It's not the easiest book I ever tackled. Maybe the most difficult . . . but Pearl, I'm convinced, the most important. I've *got* to understand it."

It wasn't clear at this point where we were headed. Except I knew that Pearl needed my help.

"Tell you what," I said, glancing at my watch, "can you join me for supper a week from Tuesday night around eight o'clock? " Eve and I had the coming Tuesday-Wednesday night weekend already tied up. "I want to hear more about these voices of yours. And I'd like to tell you more about my exchange of experiences with the two old gentlemen."

We finished our drinks, and Pearl promised me she'd not go to a shrink until we'd had a chance to talk further. I walked her home.

We met again a week from Tuesday night at eight. Pearl looked better than the last time we met. We went to a Turkish place for a some lamb stew and salad. Her problems didn't seem to stem her appetite.

"Pearl," I said, when the food had been served, "tell me about these voices."

She finished chewing a large intake of salad and wiped her mouth. The look in her eyes made me want to kiss her. The way a dad suddenly wants to comfort a child.

"I've changed my mind about the voices," she said. "I'm not ready to see a shrink, but I could use some advice from you."

I waited.

"The first time I heard a voice, medium-pitched voice, could be a man or a woman, it said: 'The nurses. Talk to the other nurses.'" She looked at me. "I turned around fast, thinking there was somebody behind me. I was in the hall, right after coming out of the operating room in Emergency. There was nobody in the hall."

She went back to the lamb stew for a few bites, looking quite calm and collected.

"Did the voice say anything else?"

"No. The first time it happened, I thought I had just imagined it. Then a couple of nights later, when I was waiting for a temperature reading, I heard it again. 'Talk to the other nurses. They'll listen. They need your help.' I looked at the patient. He hadn't heard the voice. I knew no one else was in the room. Chris, that's when I thought about my sister and maybe I was getting myself in trouble."

I patted her hand. Something I'd learned as a male nurse. Touch. Two people touching. It's may be the strongest kind of communication. Well, she lit up with a smile and went on.

"After our talk on Saturday, I realized the voice was talking about NDEs. After going through that night with Eve's sister on the table and listening to her ramble about going through the darkness, and the warm light that came toward her, and all the beautiful colors . . . well, I mentioned her experience to a friend of mine. She said she'd had a patient with the same kind of trip - in and out of death." Pearl looked away absently, then back at me. "That helped, Chris. My friend knew all about NDEs, and when I told her about the voice, she said at once that I should talk to some of the other nurses." She took another fork full of salad, chewed thoughtfully, then, "So me and her met with a couple other nurses and talked about NDEs."

She smiled, still chewing. "Chris, it's not anything new. Everyone of them had a story to tell."

A few days later, Pearl called me at the hospital and said she'd heard about a group that met once a month, Friends of IANDS. I said, "What's that?"

She explained about the organization (the International Association for Near-Death Studies), founded in 1978 and incorporated in 1981, dedicated to the study of near-death and similar experiences.

"The Friends," she said, "support the organization in various ways. They have a meeting next week. You and Eve like to go? A couple of friends, nurses, said they'd go."

"When's the meeting?"

"Friday night."

"I have to work."

She grinned. "I know. I already talked to the supervisor. When I explained it was to learn more about NDEs, she said it was time hospital staff got out in the open about what was going on. She gave you Friday night off - after six."

I shook my head. If it needed doing, if it was the way to go, trust Pearl to do it.

"Sure, Pearl. I can't say what Eve's reaction might be, but after her sister's night on the operating table . . ."

I didn't have to finish.

Pearl was nodding. "I think it was her trip that got me started - with the voice."

The following Friday, all three of us arrived at the meeting room in the YMCA at seven-thirty. We introduced ourselves to the woman who seemed to be in charge and helped ourselves to coffee and sweet rolls waiting on a table. There were only three or four others, who nodded in a friendly way and pointed to the pile of blank name tags. We filled those out, stuck them somewhere on our shirt or blouse, and sat down to wait.

Around 7:45 Pearl's friends showed up. By ten minutes to eight one more man had arrived. The lady in charge said we'd better get started and added that a few more were expected, but they might be late.

She talked for about 20 minutes, explaining what the Friends of IANDS were doing, how they made contacts with other similar groups, and then for the next 15 minutes read from a newsletter, *Vital Signs*, a long description of a lady's NDE. I was beginning to understand why some of the Friends were going to be late. They'd heard these preliminaries before.

Eve and I exchanged non-committal glances. The three nurses were not very subtle in their reactions. An occasional raised eyebrow, a slight head-shake, legs crossed and un-crossed made it clear they were hoping to hear more than another example of an NDE. I was thinking they could probably supply some good examples themselves, seeing they were usually assigned to the operating rooms.

During this slow beginning a few more people arrived, and their exchange of nods made it clear they were regulars. Their looks at us were friendly, curious, and maybe a little reserved. The thought went through my head that they belonged to a very exclusive club as NDEers, which put us on the outside looking in. Then I remembered the nurses. They were on the outside, I guess, but they were certainly "in" on the running accounts heard on the operating table.

About that time the chairperson concluded the NDE testimonial and said she was glad to welcome us newcomers, adding (I suspect based on our occasional squirming) that not all the Friends had experienced an NDE, but that anyone interested in the subject was welcome. I guess that was a kind of blanket assurance that whether we belonged to the club or not, we were among friends - Friends of IANDS.

A woman in her late 30s spoke up. "I haven't had an NDE, but my Charlotte did." She patted the hand of a girl about 16 sitting next to her. "It changed our lives," she said. "Mine more than hers. She was already kind and considerate of everybody else. *I'm* the one," the mother added, "who was shocked into a new life. When I got Charlotte back from the grave, my own flesh and blood, it completely changed my life. It made me know I was a self-centered flirt all my life, more interested in me than anything else. In fact, I went with a pretty fast crowd." She paused. "Into hard drugs."

She looked around the room, as though somebody might comment. "I haven't seen any of them since the night I thought I had lost my Charlotte. I prayed. First time in my life, I prayed. I'm a new person. I learned that giving is receiving. Helping, even with little things, is knowing real peace. Contentment. Fulfillment. That started more than a year ago. I spend a lot of time with my daughter." She smiled and looked around at the rest of us. "That makes me, the new me, not much more than a year old. Huh, Charlotte."

Her daughter studied her hands.

The chairperson thanked her and turned to the first person seated on her left. "Dan, several of us haven't been here before. Will you start us around the room with a few words about yourself?"

Thinking about Bob and Tom and Clair I wondered how they would handle this. I only half-listened to the recital of the first three people, stories of how they got interested, the first one with a psychic experience, which he said was waking up in the middle of the night to see his dead father standing at the foot of the bed. He was smiling and pointing to a closet. A letter found under some boxes was his father's will, explaining why he had chosen suicide. The second person was a young woman about Eve's age, who had a friend, not present, whose NDE had changed both their lives and cemented a friendship. The third was a middle-aged man curious to know more about Ouiji boards and table tipping. Then it was my turn.

I explained that accidentally I'd met these two old gentlemen, who knew people like Stewart Edward White and Dr. J. B. Rhine at Duke University and had corresponded with Edgar Casey. I said that I'd read some of the New Age publications and saw a need for more than descriptions of these wonderful experiences. The things the two old men talked about and the books they recommended explained some of the unanswered questions raised in New Age publications. "In other words," I said, "these early writers said a lot that will be a help to IANDS." I hesitated. "And to the Friends of IANDS."

168

I paused and looked around. "Do some of you recognize those names? Maybe you've read some of their books?"

One person had heard the name, Stewart Edward White, but hadn't read any of the Betty books. No one had heard of J.B. Rhine, but when I mentioned "the Department of Parapsychology at Duke" and "ESP," one woman nodded. An older man had heard of Edgar Casey but didn't know much about him.

I didn't think I was getting through to them. "The oldest gentleman is an entomologist, knows a lot about bugs and plants. He hold five patents, has written more than 100 articles and is in the *Men of Science* publication."

I waited. There was no reaction. "His wife," I rushed on, "was also in the university, medical research and teaching. She's gone on beyond the NDE phase and communicates with us from the other side." This remark got few "ohs." "The other old gentleman," I added, "is in the university arts and humanities - world music."

Eve gave me an almost imperceptible slight head shake. So I decided I had said enough.

She was next. "My kid sister had a bad accident. On the operating table she had a Near Death Experience."

The chairperson said, "Wonderful! Maybe you can bring her to our next meeting"

Eve stared at the chairperson a moment. "It's only been a few weeks Maybe when she can walk again.. I'll ask her."

I listened to the nurses, who gave short reports of things they'd heard in the operating room. Pearl was the third one to speak and said a few things about Eve's sister's experience.

"If she comes to one of your meetings, maybe she'll talk about it." Pearl looked at the chairperson. "I think she was the sixth one I've heard describe an NDE during an operation. No two were the same. But they had things in common." She took a deep breath and looked around the table. "One man told me later he was frightened."

The rest of the evening was more of the same. How they had a psychic experience, what they learned from an NDE, how it changed their way of looking at life, and helped them understand they could lead better lives.

A young man said, "I guess knowing somebody who had an NDE made me realize that everyone is conscious, you know what happens to you. That's the one thing you can be sure of - you're conscious.

I couldn't keep still. "That's it! That's what it's all about. Consciousness. The one and only thing each of us can be sure of. My two old friends say it's the I AM principle."

Except for an exchange of glances around the room there was no reaction.

I glanced at Eve; she was looking off into space. We sure were going to have a long talk about the evening. I looked from face-to-face. There were no Tonys the ditch digger. And for sure no Einsteins. Just ordinary people like Pearl and Eve and me. They had hold of something that meant a lot to them. But it was all a little vague. If only they could know the two old gentlemen and read some the older books. I found myself wondering if maybe that was something *I* was supposed to do. Find ways to get some of the Friends to read the Betty books, *The Unobstructed Universe*, J. B. Rhine's publications, meet Bob and hear about things the scientists were doing.

During the next hour I said little but listened carefully to the others. One person's rambling account of voices heard, of white lights that serve as psychic "shields," of things that go "bump in the night" . . . well, I got to studying the other faces for reactions. The recital was vague, uncertain, sometimes contradictory, but it sounded sincere. Especially when she talked about her guiding spirit, a presence she felt constantly around her. Several heads nodded. Was she talking about a "guardian angel?"

Yes, those sessions at the library exchanging experiences with two old men and Clair could help these Friends a lot - if I could figure out how to get their ideas across and get the Friends reading some of the basic books. But that was as tough as trying to figure out what my baseball dream was all about. Like trying to spell "night" with an "e."

It was easy just to listen. The more people talked, the more talkative they became. I had the feeling some of their talk wasn't really communicating. There seemed to be more talking than listening. I got to thinking about those visits to the park, before our meetings at the library. The continual flow of words got me wondering what the Friends would say, if I told them scientists have proved that trees can communicate with one another.

After the meeting was over, the chairperson came up to me. "Chris, I'd like to meet your man who is involved with world music." She looked around to be sure our conversation was private. "Chris, we're all alike. Everywhere in the whole world. But I'm suspicious of words. I trust the look of eyes. The way people move and relate to one another. I've always believed that music is the most honest form of communication. We learn a lot about people, getting to know their native music and folk dances. I've got an old acquaintance in Appalachia. He's probably the biggest liar I know, when he's telling tales. But when he plays the fretless five-string banjo, that's different. You can lie with words, but you can't lie with music or dance."

Now I had something to carry back to our next Tuesday meeting with Bob and Tom and Clair. Then I remembered the woman's insistence that it was her guiding spirit who was with her all the time and looked after her. I wondered what our Tuesday night trio might be able to tell us about that.

Chapter XXIX

THE NEXT TUESDAY, Eve and I skipped the park and went directly to the seminar room in the library. Bob and Tom hadn't arrived yet, so I thought it would be a good time to sound out Eve's reaction to the meeting of the Friends of IANDS. That Friday night after the meeting, it was nearly eleven before we reached her apartment. She said she was bushed, so we didn't talk about the Friends.

Eve sat in my lounge chair again, so I pulled up the straight-back.

"They'll be along soon," I said for openers, "maybe we can spend a few minutes on that gathering with the Friends. Have you had time to think about it?"

"No, not really. There wasn't a lot to think about. Most of it was telling about things that had happened to them. No talk about what it meant, why it happened, what it meant for the future." She hesitated. "Don't get me wrong, Chris. They were honest and sincere. I guess they belong to the Friends, because they've all got things in common."

I thought about that. People you've got things in common with. I guess that was the definition of all kinds of friends. "Eve, that little lady who talked about white lights and premonitions and hunches. I was with her until she mentioned her guiding spirit. Somebody or 'some thing' - she was very vague about that - who was around all the time. At least on call all the time Her guiding spirit. What do you think she meant by her 'guiding spirit?'"

She gave me a quick you-mean-you-didn't-get-it look. "Guiding spirit, guardian angel," Eve said, "that's not a new idea."

"She didn't say 'angel.'"

"Okay, 'spirit.'"

"You think it's what you Catholics call a guardian angel?"

Eve looked thoughtful in her hesitation, as though she was pondering a choice. "When she talked about it, it seemed clear she was talking about her guardian angel." She paused again. "Now, when I think about some of other things she said, I'm not so sure that guiding spirit means the same thing to her that guardian angel does to me."

I thought I'd test the water. "Could she be referring to a guiding animal spirit? I've heard of such things."

Eve's shrugged, as Bob and Tom entered. After a greeting, they pulled up their chairs, and Bob leaned forward.

"Your sister, is she okay? Getting over the accident?"

"It's been difficult. The death of her boyfriend, and what happened to her leg. But, yes, she's doing fine. In fact, she' doing better than she has in a long time. She's more positive about things, not exactly cheerful, but more at peace with herself. And everybody else."

I was ready to tell them about the Friday night meeting. "Eve and I went to a meeting. The Friends of IANDS. Ever heard of it?"

"Oh, yes."

Bob's quick response was reassuring.

"Know anything about them?"

"The Friends?" Tom was nodding. "They seem to be an honest group trying to understand NDEs and the meaning of such an experience."

"Do you think they know the early publications of people like White and Dr. Rhine?"

Tom's glance was directed to Bob. "We've wondered about that. I suspect they don't."

"I can vouch for that. At the meeting of the Friends only one person had ever heard of Stewart Edward White, and he hadn't read any of his books. Nobody knew Dr. Rhine's name, much less his publications. One person had heard of the terms 'parapsychology' and 'ESP,' but didn't say what they meant."

Bob was nodding. "I talked to one or two in IANDS and have written to several authors of New Age publications. So far as I know, no one has followed up on my suggestions. Maybe it's because most of the early publications are out of print, and interlibrary loan is more trouble than buying a book."

"I understand that," I said. "Eve found a copy of *The Unobstructed Universe* for me, but it's only good for three weeks. Pretty heavy reading for that short time."

Eve caught Bob's eye. "One lady talked about her guiding spirit. I thought she meant her guardian angel. Chris wonders whether it was some other kind of spirit. Maybe even an animal. Can you tell us, Bob?"

"If she meant guardian angel, she would have said so. 'Guiding spirit' might be any kind. Animal spirits are common among Native Americans and Alaskans. Tom, tell them about some of the ideas you've met in your travels."

Tom's brow was furrowed. "I'll try. I can report what I've seen and heard. Explanations are something else."

He was silent for a minute, a habit of his when he was trying to boil something down to a brief story. We waited.

"I lived in Hawaii for a number of years," he said, "and one or two experiences during that time might be pertinent. I was working on a musical drama based on historical accounts of Hawaii. The more digging I did the more I realized that, like most histories, some names had been glorified to cover the naked truth. To get the best objective information I worked for a time with Maui's historian."

He laughed. "No, I won't get sidetracked on Hawaiian history. But an experience with the historian is worth hearing. We had been on the Hana side of Maui, meeting old Hawaiians, visiting a taro-patch farmer and his family, where two teenage girls lived. They sang for me. Old songs, accompanying themselves on the ukulele. One long song I was very privileged to hear, because there was clear musical evidence it predated arrival of the Yale missionaries.

"Sorry," he laughed again, "that's still not my story. We were driving down a macadam road, the historian pointing out landmarks and telling tales associated with them, when suddenly about twenty feet in front of the car there was an owl. It was early afternoon. I said to her, 'Look at that owl! I never saw one flying around in the middle of the afternoon.'

"She smiled, and we continued to watch fascinated, because the owl was flying just ahead of the car at the same speed we were traveling. 'Look!' I said again, 'that owl thinks he leading us!' The road was winding and for nearly a mile and a half the owl continued to lead us.

"I was puzzled that the historian made no comment. She had a smile on her face, as though she knew something about owls I didn't know. After the owl flew off in a different direction, I continued to listen to the historian point out things she thought I'd be interested in. She had read the script for my musical and was anxious that I learn as much as possible to help set history straight."

Tom thought for a minute, then continued. "She lived with her husband in Wailuku, the capitol of Maui. He was sitting on the front porch looking out over the bay, watching the surfers. She introduced us. 'He'll tell you about the great *tsunami* that flooded Wailuku years ago. We watched from our porch.' Then she said, 'But first there's something in the bedroom I want to show you.'

"I followed her into the house. We went into a small bedroom, and she walked over to the top drawer of a dresser and pulled it out. 'Look,' she said. I looked into the large drawer, and there was every imaginable depiction of owls, carved out of wood, ivory, rock, lava. I picked up several of them and turned to her with my eyes asking the question. 'My *amakua*,' she said simply, 'my guiding spirit all my life.'"

I'd never see an owl fly in mid afternoon. And now I was hearing that some owls are guiding spirits. Eve and I exchanged looks.

Tom went on. "I heard about guiding spirits in another way," he was saying. "When I lived in Hawaii, I was in a large house built in pavilion style. Some nights, in the bedroom pavilion, I heard what sounded like bare feet walking on hollow wooden planks. Some sounded like a heavy tread, some were lighter. The house was in a neighborhood where almost everyone had a swimming pool. Mine did not. The first few times I heard those sounds, I supposed it was late bathers in the immediate neighborhood, walking on their decking. Finally one night I got out of bed and went outside to investigate. But when I got there, the sounds had stopped. There were no lights on any neighbor's pool. I went back to bed."

He paused for a deep sigh. "Well, that little exercise was repeated several times, and each time, when I was outside the sounds stopped, and there were no bathers in neighboring swimming pools. Then one night, sitting on the lanai gazing at our little Japanese garden, I heard the footsteps again. This time, outside. No bedroom, no possible echoing walls. I guess you've heard the phrase, 'little hairs stood up on the back of my neck.' After a few minutes the sounds stopped."

"Did you figure it out," I asked.

"I asked a Hawaiian friend about it. He said the ground my house was on had been a special area facing Manalua Bay where Hawaiian royalty lived, long before the English ships came to Oahu and put into the Bay to get fresh water. What I was hearing, he said, were *lapu, huaka'i po,* royal processions. He said they were friendly spirits, but if I'd feel better I should hire a *kahuna nui* to bless the land. The *kahuna* would know how to bring rest to the wandering souls."

Tom was silent, as though waiting for our reaction.

"And did you hire a whatever you call him - a Hawaiian priest, I guess?"

Tom nodded. "And the sounds stopped." He was smiling. "After the fact, I thought maybe I'd made a mistake. I missed their company." He turned to Eve and said, "You're Catholic, right Eve?"

She nodded. "Sort of."

"I was thinking of another kind of spirits I learned about in Bali."

Eve sat up straight. "Balinese Catholics?"

He laughed. "No, no. Balinese Hindus. They have a belief that reminds me of the Catholic concept of 'purgatory.' Wandering souls that have led troubled lives, right?"

"Something like that."

"In Bali the traditional dwelling is pavilion-style, with a wall surrounding the entire property. According to Balinese Hinduism three shrines or outdoor altars, must be built; two within the walls, one outside the walls. The biggest and most impressive, usually has its own wall enclosure and is built in honor of the supreme god - Shiva, Dewarutji; the second one slightly smaller is built to honor

177

the protective spirits of the ancestors and the spirits of the land; a third one, the smallest, is built outside the walls surrounding the dwelling place to appease the restless spirits who have led troubled lives. Offerings of flower petals, rice, and simple foods are placed before each altar every day."

He looked at Eve. "The third one, I suggest, has a meaning similar to your term 'purgatory.'"

I was thinking of the chairperson at the meeting of the Friends. "The woman leading the meeting of the friends said we're all alike. Catholics, Balinese Hindus - very different in some ways, but about the same in their belief in purgatory."

Tom spoke up again. "One more example, if you like. This one very short and from Africa. A few years ago, I lived in Ghana among the Ashanti making a film. Almost every night I drove back from the village where I was filming to Kumasi, the old Ashanti capitol where I could recharge the camera batteries. Some evenings the Chief of that area caught a ride with me. Every time, just before we went over a bridge spanning a small stream, he would yell, '*honk! honk the horn! keep honking!*' until we had crossed the bridge. The third time that happened, when I realized there had been no threat to anyone on the road, I asked the Chief why the honking was necessary. 'To scare away the evil spirits who live in the water,' was his answer."

For maybe three or four minutes we just sat in silence, each of us, I guess, thinking our own thoughts about spirits, good or bad.

Finally Bob said,. "I think Clair has some thoughts we might want to hear." He paused, then went on speaking in the style of thought we recogized as Clair's.

"Those who believe in guiding spirits and/or guardian angels must not be denied. They are believers of a religion of choice that may or may not include such entities as guiding spirits and/or guardian angels, as well as a deity of their own, who serve equally as their protector. All are entitled to a spiritual protector of choice, and each should respect the choice of another. Each should stay with the spiritual protector they feel most comforted with.

"Admittedly some denominations take their spiritual protectors more seriously than others. They, too, are entitled to their devotion. Suffice it to say that all religions of the world teach the presence of a higher authority that protects those who believe in their existence. This, too, must never be denied.

"We who exist in the Unobstructed Universe take a more universal view of who is not responsible for the lives and well being of those who still exit in the obstructed phase of our one and only universe. We teach that each obstructed individual is responsible for his or her own life with one exception: children - those too young to know the difference between safety and danger. They, we watch over and help whenever possible, short of cataclysmic acts of nature that occur unexpectedly. Even these we are aware of with full realization that such acts are a part of natural balance, as are necessary 'rides' of the Four Horsemen of the Apocalypse."

We let that sink in for a minute, then I asked Tom, "Do you have one of those guiding spirits?"

He looked at me with a different expression on his face. "You mean, do I have an *amakua*?"

I nodded.

For several minutes I didn't think he was going to answer me. Then he said, "Yes, Chris, ever since I was seven. That's when my father died. I used to hike two miles to the grave site and just sit and think. Sometimes cry. A lone dove was always there. Not two doves - they mate for life, you know - but one dove. By now there have been so many sudden appearances of one dove it would take too long to list them." He hesitated. "It was not until 50 years later I learned from Maui's historian that I, too, have an *amakua*.

Eve was looking at me in a way that suddenly registered. I had promised we'd leave early, so she could be with her sister Joan.

I thanked Tom for telling us his experiences, we said goodnight to the two of them, and left the seminar room.

We never saw them again.

Chapter XXX

THE FOLLOWING SATURDAY, when I got to the hospital at four, Pearl caught me by the elbow as I came in through the swinging doors.

"Chris," she said, "the CEO wants to see you."

"Dr. Kendall?" My mouth went dry. The famous Dr. Kendall was almost a myth at the hospital. Ever since we merged with the new HMO, he was the top executive of everything in the hospital. He was so much in demand, few of us ever caught a glimpse of him. He got his reputation as a surgeon. No time for operations these days. "Wonder what I've done wrong. Where do I go?"

"Fifth floor, where the executive suites are."

All the way up to the fifth floor I kept worrying. *The* Dr. Kendall! I'd seen him once or twice at a distance, when somebody pointed him out. I didn't think he even knew my name. I knew he didn't. Male nurse in Emergency. Maybe I was about to become a male nurse without a job.

When I entered the suite, the secretary smiled as I gave my name at the desk. "Oh, Chris. Please take a chair. Dr. Kendall should be free in a few minutes."

After two tries I found my voice. "Excuse me, Miss. Do you know what it's about?"

I couldn't tell whether her smile had become friendly, sympathetic, or just annoyed. "We'd better let Dr. Kendall discuss that with you."

The magazine on the end table was three months old and featured political news that by now was ridiculous. The rumors had been blown away by counter charges more scandalous than the rumors. I noticed a brochure explaining several new costly plans for which the HMO urged enrollment. I tried reading them.

After 25 minutes, the secretary called from her desk. "Just a few more minutes, Chris."

Well, the hell with their damned job! There were other hospitals in Boston. A good male nurse was always in demand. Especially one who had some training in med school. So I convinced myself I didn't really care what the great Dr. Kendall might say. I was still amazed that a VIP like him would bother with a nobody like me. Wait a minute! Had I done something wrong that might get me in trouble? I had always been very careful with anything connected with radio-active waste. What had I done wrong? I was sweating.

Saturday afternoon, 4:30. What a helluva way to start a Saturday night on duty for Emergency. I asked the secretary where I could get a drink of water.

There was a buzz on the intercom. "Dr. Kendall can see you now she said. You still need that drink?"

I shook my head and went to the door she was holding open.

As I crossed the room, Dr. Kendall got out of his chair behind the desk and came around to shake hands. He was short, almost stubby, very overweight, with a round face and steely blue eyes. In another surrounding he could be mistaken for a bar tender or a used-car salesman Any profession not related to proper diet and exercise. His hands were something else. Strong, firm, neatly trimmed, the hands of a surgeon. "You're Chris!"

I nodded. I couldn't manage a smile but did manage to sink into the chair he was pointing to. He sat in the one opposite, both of them at the front of his desk. "We've been hearing about you."

I was wishing I had got that drink of water. My mouth was so dry I kept swallowing. Hearing about me. I waited.

"The helpers in Emergency have been telling us about you."

Now it was "us" - whoever made up reports about personnel.

"I'm told you've taken all your classes for paramedic."

I finally found my voice. "About another month to go," I said.

"That's good to get all that behind you. And you went through most of med school, right?"

"Some. I had to drop out because of money."

"Uhuh. Well, the reports have been good, Chris, mighty good. We're glad you've been part of our team."

There it was! Softening me up for the kill. The past tense brought my heart right up into my throat. Pretty slick CEO, firing me with faint praise. But I was still puzzled why this giant executive of a giant industry was bothering to talk to *me*. The Supervisor on the first floor could fire me.

I got to my feet, wondering whether I should try to make a short speech. But about what? He was still seated.

"Keep your chair, Chris. I want to explain why you're leaving us."

I sat down again, clamped my mouth shut, and waited.

He reached for a pack of cigarettes on his desk and offered me one. I shook my head.

He smiled. "It's been open four months. Only five gone. All to teenagers."

At least he didn't smoke.

"I quit and thought an open pack on the desk would make a good test. It has been - I've learned where the market is."

His smile vanished.

"The Chief of Police is an old classmate of mine - I was in pre-law for a while. When we were at Johns Hopkins."

I was too frightened even to swallow.

His second smile. "The interns and nurses in Emergency say you've got a special touch. Manage to look past the carnage and see the patient, talk to him, keep him alive while everybody's struggling with sutures and sedatives. You seem to have that inside calm that means a good doctor. Let me come to the point."

Dr. Kendall reached back to his desk and picked up a card. "The Chief ask me to recommend someone to serve as a regular paramedic in his emergency-helicopter crew. I told him about you. Interested?"

I knew my head was nodding up and down, but I couldn't speak.

"He wants you to report for work right away. This afternoon. They've got a regular patrol above the six o'clock traffic. If you go now," he handed me the card, "you can start with them right away. And good luck!"

He bounced to his feet, shook hands with me again, and turned back to his desk.

I realized I'd been dismissed.

"Thanks," I said and stumbled out the door.

The secretary's smile looked to me like a slice of heaven. "Pays good, too!" she whispered.

I didn't stop for the elevator, but ran down the stairs, spotted Pearl waiting by the swinging doors. "Paramedic!" I shouted, gave her a hug, and burst through the doors to find a cab. Wow! What a beautiful Saturday afternoon.

In the taxi I handed the cabbie the card. "Can you get me there before six?"

"With Boston traffic at this hour?"

I fished out a 20-dollar bill.

He stuffed it into his shirt pocket and said, "We'll make it."

We made it.

Meeting the pilot of the 'copter, the copilot, checking through the box of emergency medical supplies, listening to the deafening roar as we took off from the roof of the building, out over parking lots, bumper-to-bumper traffic, hearing the staccato chatter from the intercom - what a way to start a new job! It was all a blur of newness that made me so pumped up with excitement I thought I might hyperventilate.

The copilot, Ned, was a young guy, maybe in his mid 20s. His eyes and grin were friendly. "You new at this?" he yelled over the whir of overhead blades.

I nodded and grinned back. We were passing above the slow heavy traffic and began to pick speed as we moved toward a distant broad artery that skirted the edge of downtown traffic. The pilot was nodding in response to something coming over his headphones. I heard him say, "We should be able to spot 'em in a couple of minutes."

"How long do we cruise like this?" I asked Ned.

184

"Until we see something that needs our attention."

"Like?"

"An accident . . . excessive speeding . . . anything law breakers might do."

I watched the passing scenery down below and remembered my dream. There it was again, little cars, small houses, tiny people. Then suddenly I stared at the three-lane highway below and heard the words: "This is important! Remember this!" It was the same scene! There they were! Five squad cars chasing a black panel truck! I tapped the copilot on the shoulder and pointed.

He nodded and said over the noise. "We're on our way down to take a closer look."

As we dropped down several hundred feet, until we were above the speeding cars, I saw motorists moving the opposite direction looking up at the sound of the helicopter. *They were looking up!* The copilot pointed to the black panel truck, only a few hundred feet below us. "They hear us. If they're smart, they'll slow down."

We were moving above the car at the same speed. Suddenly it spurted ahead. It began weaving in and out of traffic that was becoming heavier as we moved. The squad cars had picked up speed, but stayed behind the truck, as though uncertain whether to try to pull ahead of it. Faintly we could hear their sirens above the sound of the helicopter.

Ned had pulled an AK47 into his lap, watching every dangerous swerve of the black panel truck.

"They're gonna crash!" I said to no one.

It was a nightmare. Lotsa people were looking up at us now. Drivers of cars on the highway who could hear the sirens were pulling over to the right and left aprons to allow the speeding cars to pass. I guessed we were moving close to 100 miles an hour.

The driver of a large oil truck in response to the sirens started to pull over to the right lane. The black panel truck had just swerved left, and then abruptly, to compensate the dangerous sway of his turn, pulled back to the right. It smashed into the right rear side of the oil truck, and almost at once there was an explosion with flames so high the heat waves made the 'copter bounce.

The squad cars swerved to the left and narrowly missed the burning wreckage piling up on the right apron.

Ned put the AK47 back in its rack. "Won't need this," he said, as the helicopter checked its speed and began circling for a place to land.

On the ground Ned handed me a fireproof vest and gloves, pointing to the box of medical supplies. "Bring it. If we get the driver out in time, you may be able to help him."

The driver of the oil truck got out safely and in a daze was standing several hundred feet beyond the wreck, watching the flames shoot skyward. Ned and I with our heat shields in front of us got to the driver of the panel truck. A pinch bar broke open the jammed driver's door, and we managed to pull a man out of the burning car, his clothes on fire and his face mashed flat and pierced with glass. We carried the body to one side and turned to warn people to stay back from the burning trucks.

That was my first assignment as a paramedic - getting acquainted with a body bag.

Back at Police Headquarters I tried to phone Eve. But she was out. On her answering service I said, "I've changed jobs, Eve. Tell you about it later." I thought of calling Bob and Tom, but decided it all could wait until Tuesday night, after the Park, in the seminar room of the library.

This time I really had an experience to exchange! A new job and the beginning of understanding my "remember-this" dream. I wondered how much more I'd understand in 20 years.

Chapter XXXI

TUESDAY EVENING PROMPTLY at seven o'clock, Eve and I were in the Park, waiting for Bob and Tom. The air was crisp, hinting at Fall weather to come. The leaves on Bob's dogwood were dark green and full; one or two had turned yellow. The other dogwood was looking bad. Many of the leaves had curled and were brown; several lower branches appeared to be dead, the leaves dry and shriveled up.

Eve looked at it wistfully. "If we ever plant a dogwood, Chris, be sure to ask Bob what to say to it. What a difference between the two!"

I had managed to give her the good news of my job first by phone, then, when I took her out to late dinner on Monday, I filled in some of the details,. My new schedule kept me busy weekends, three other afternoons, and early evenings. Monday and Tuesday were days off.

On Monday, when I had told her about my jump in salary and asked when we could pick out an engagement ring, she gave me a long, warm kiss. Then with eyes shinning, she said, "I guess you're asking me to marry you. And I guess I'm saying yes." She gave me another quick kiss. "I'll ask for a free day tomorrow. We'll do our shopping, have dinner, and go to the Park, where I can show off my new ring to Bob and Tom."

Now, in the Park, she was glancing at it every few minutes. It wasn't showy, not very big, but it was a good quality diamond.

The jeweler gave us a written guarantee to take it back at full price any time within a year, which sounded like a pretty solid deal.

We were both a little heady. New job, new ring, new future . . . people and things were definitely looking up. "Eve, that view from the helicopter I told you about was my 'this-is-important' dream, the squad cars chasing a black panel truck."

"I remember."

"As we got lower above the truck, *everybody was looking up* at the helicopter."

She nodded. "You already told me that."

"But I didn't tell you what I heard on TV last night. The number of people going back to church has been growing fast. People are beginning to turn back to religion, looking for answers to their society out-of-control. Eve," I looked into her eyes, "don't you get it? Pretty soon *almost everyone will be looking up*. That's the next phase of my dream."

When I first told her about the new job, I had made the end of the story short, so we wouldn't be dwelling on a sad ending. I didn't find out what the panel truck had been running from until the next day. Ned told me the truck was loaded with hard drugs.

Eve and I sat on a bench, she eyeing her ring, I remembering that my paramedic job had started off with a body bag.

I noticed it was nearly seven-twenty. "Maybe they're going directly to the seminar room.. We'd better take off for the library."

Twenty minutes later we were in the seminar room. No Bob or Tom.

We sat in the lounge chairs. I was intending to yield mine when they came. After a few minutes, Eve said, "Let me ask at the desk. Maybe they left a message for us."

She was gone about five minutes, then walked in with a shake of her head. "No note."

We sat back in the lounge chairs. I said, "That's really not like them. They wouldn't fail to show up without a word, some explanation. I don't understand.'

After another ten minutes, I stood up. "Be right back, Eve. I've got their phone number. Maybe one of them is sick."

I went to the pay phone, dropped in a quarter, and waited for the ring. It didn't ring. A recorded voice came on, recited the number twice and said it was no longer in service.. After a five second pause, the whole message was repeated. I decided to get the general supervisor and find out when it had been disconnected.

Back in the seminar room, when Eve heard about the recorded message, we sat silent for maybe five minutes.

"Chris, you have their address?"

"I only talked with Tom twice by phone. He never gave me their address. He said it was not far from here."

"Chris . . . how old do you think Bob and Tom are?"

"I don't know. They didn't say." I was remembering some of the things they had talked about. "In their late 70s or 80s, I'd guess. But to hear them talk it sounded more like their 60s. Why?"

"Remember their discussions that led us to the conclusion that everybody is here on this earth to do a job? Often those who experience an NDE say their job wasn't finished. And that's why they were allowed to come back."

Eve always thought faster than I did. "So?"

"Maybe Bob and Tom - and Clair had a job to finish up. Maybe they've done it. Maybe we were it."

Suddenly I had a flushed sensation. Maybe something like the tingles Bob always talked about. I was remembering that early in our Friday night exchange of experiences Bob told me Clair was a powerful force "bringing us all together . . . you, too, Chris."

I looked at her. "You mean . . . we were their job? Teaching us the meaning of I AM, the phases of consciousness, quantity here, quality in the unobstructed universe?"

Eve was looking at me in a way I hadn't seen before. "They found a male nurse who hadn't figured out what he was doing with his life. When Tom met him waiting for a train, he got him interested. After a few more meetings, the male nurse began to know not only who he is but what he has to do. Then there's this Catholic member of the laity who wasn't ready for all this. She's ready now. And Chris," her eyes had a new depth, "my sister Joan got through her NDE and understood."

I thought about that for several minutes. "And?"

"Their work's finished. Wherever they are. Now it's our turn."

We sat for another few minutes, both of us wrapped up in our own thoughts about Bob, Tom, and Clair.

Finally Eve stood up. "Chris, I want to show the other librarians my ring. You want to come along?"

I stood up. "Sure, Eve. I'll join you at the front desk in a few minutes. I want to check the New Age section to see if I can find a book the lady mentioned at the Friends meeting."

We walked to the door together. "See you in a few minutes," I said, and she went off toward the main desk.

When she was out of sight, I went back into the seminar room and sat in one of the lounge chairs, the one Bob had occupied. I looked at the other one in which Tom usually sat. I got up and sat in the one I used before Eve joined us, and looked back at the other two chairs.

I hadn't told Eve what I learned from the general supervisor on the telephone. She said that telephone number had not been in use for many months.

Then I remembered my question to Tom, when we were waiting for the subway train. "Do you believe in ghosts?"

And his answer: "Only those I've seen or talked with."
